MAGNIFICAT

MAGNIFICAT

By

RENÉ BAZIN

NEW YORK

THE MACMILLAN COMPANY

1932

PRINTED IN THE UNITED STATES OF AMERICA, BY THE
NATIONAL PROCESS COMPANY, INC., NEW YORK, N. Y.

CONTENTS

MAGNIFICAT

CHAPTER I

THE PENMUR HOUSEHOLD

JEAN-GUILLAUME MAGUERN let fall the rope of the young heifer which he had just bought. The blustering winter wind compelled him to give his whole attention to his old-fashioned Breton hat. To prevent this from being wrenched away, he jammed the black felt hard upon his head and tied the velvet strings.

' Now,' he muttered, ' if the wind wants to blow off my hat, it must blow my head off too ! '

He turned to find the heifer grazing upon the short grass of the hill-side. Whimsically he said to her : ' We're both in the same boat, old girl. That's it—have a bite to eat. The lady at Grand Néant won't mind— she's a real lady, she is.'

He began to clamber upward and soon reached the moor. On a hillock stood a new house built wholly of granite. No kitchen-garden stretched behind it. No flower-beds lent beauty to its front, nor was there trace of borders with promise of flowers to come.

The house dominated that part of the moor. On the side where the heifer now grazed were meadows sloping

down to a remote and narrow road. Beyond the stretch
of moor were the home fields of Grand Néant (in its
local Breton form, Grand Néan : the wide horizon), the
farm hidden in the trees on the slope. Even as late as
thirty years back the whole hill-side and much of the
land in the valley had been altogether wild, given over
to furze and broom and heath through whose tangled
growth a few ferns struggled towards the light.

It was a wide-stretching country-side. Jean-Guillaume
stood gazing towards the south where he knew the house
to be. The undulating landscape seemed to fade into
infinity, to those who did not know that the sinking sun
was still shining over the chopping invisible sea.

It was a country-side of blunt tilled hillocks. The
darker shadows marked deep and winding valleys with
brisk-running nameless rivers. These valleys sheltered
the trees whose rich beauty was the richer for their great
variety—the trees which could gain no foothold on the
higher land, swept as it was by autumn storms and winter
gales. Nevertheless, here a clump of pines, there a
straggling file of them, now a solitary tree stood
silhouetted upon this crest or upon that, challenging
heaven with defiant branches. The south wind might
blow or the north or the east ; the pines bent before
none of them. A branch might break ; its fellows
stood firm.

The man knew all these trees and every farm they
sheltered. As he caught sight of the slate or thatched
roofs scattered over that lonely country-side he murmured their names to himself. Grand Néant came first,
home of the handsome Le Pallec family ; then Kerantar,
where the Pocreau folk lived ; Kerlan, belonging to the
Roberts ; Trébon, the Savarys' house ; Hinzal and

Bréotty, perched on the steep- cliffs of Penmur Pool, from whose high threshing-floors wisps of chaff went fluttering down to the water like spray in the wind.

On this particular evening it was a country-side grown tranquil, unstirring save for the characteristically high wind which worked no havoc, despite its strength. Here and there patches of mist hung low over the fields, their vapour grey against the black earth. The only sound came from the north. It was a sound of rumbling, the rumbling of trains with their loads of men, munitions and supplies. For the war had already lasted seventeen months.

From his high vantage-point Maguern saw the sudden flashing of the great lantern of Goulphar lighthouse at distant Belle-Île. Regularly its long rays lit the gathering darkness. Jean-Guillaume picked up the cord of the tether-rope and led his beast down the sloping meadows. Soon he left the country road for a path across the fields, branching off upon a track whose gates he swung back that the heifer might pass. They reached the high moorland bounded by two streams that, rising at Questembert, fell between perpendicular cliffs into the lake known as Penmur Pool, the pool at the head of the sea. In front of the farm was close-cropped pasture land descending abruptly at the further end towards the unseen waters. A clump of bushes leaning in the wind marked the bend of the road, which turned into the farmyard. To the left was the farm itself, an ancient straggling building sloping down to the pool. At this late hour it stood dark save for a glimmer in one of the windows.

Jean-Guillaume shortened the lead rope and grasped

the animal's horns to prevent it from falling in the slush and the broken stones. With a vigorous thrust he pushed open one side of the double door near the end of the farm buildings. The smell of cattle and the muted lowing of the disturbed beasts greeted the farmer as he went to the end of the long line of oxen and milch-cows where he knew there was an empty stall. Grop-ingly he led the new heifer to the back of the cattle house and tied it to a post with a trough in front of it and a feeding-rack above.

The clatter of his clogs on the threshold of the brightly lit living-room warned the family of Jean-Guillaume's return. The children rose to their feet, and in voices of varying shrillness cried : ' Evening, father.'

' Evening, all of you. It's a black night out. The heifer was nearly dead beat. I thought we should never get here.'

The children, the youngest at the lower end, were in their usual places on one side of the table, above which hung a shaded oil lamp with a copper bowl. In its light their round young faces shone like so many red and golden apples. They were waiting for supper, which the women were busy preparing. As the farmer came in, they had momentarily stopped their work. He seated himself heavily at the top of the table by the side of his tall son Gildas. The children's mother, a strong active woman, held a frying-pan in her right hand and a fork in her left to stir the eggs, which she was stirring, and to prevent them from sticking to the pan.

Denise, wife of Pol, the eldest Maguern boy, who was then in the trenches near Verdun, had an authority at the farm second only to her mother-in-law's. She was matronly, though hers was a melancholy matronhood.

Busy in fetching cider from the cellar, she went to and fro, at each short journey setting the jars on the table.

Finally, there was Anna, the daughter of Jean-Guillaume's elder brother. She acted as servant to the family. It was she who set plate, fork, and spoon for each of them. They all gave her a friendly word or glance : ' Good evening, Anna ! '—' Anna, it's good to see your smile ! '—' I've got a fine old hunger, Anna ; have you ? '—' Go and warm your hands at the fire, Anna : they're as cold as the plates ! '

These remarks were from the younger children. Gildas, unlike the rest, said nothing, but looked a little longer than they at the girl as she set his place. She was not slow to understand that his liking for her was warmer than that of the others.

She made no conscious response to his look, and continued her serving without a pause. Yet as she turned to take new plates from the rack, her face expressed her deep joy in sharing so warm a friendship. She was a trifle older than her cousin—surely no matter for regret with a pair so young, nor any obstacle to first love.

Except for the youngest, Alexis, a small and sickly child, all who lived at Penmur farm had the health which goes with old and unmixed Breton blood, itself as vitalising as the Breton moors. Anna was an example of the race at its purest and best. As she moved about the room her dreaming eyes with their lowered lids were like those of a girl in unbroken prayer. Her head had the long line and her neck the long curve of an aristocrat. Her complexion, less rose than gold, had a quiet beauty, and her eyebrows were attractive with their soft, scarcely visible arches. Something of her soul's quality was expressed in her maternal air and in her moods that could quickly turn to tenderness. If a word or a single glance from those she served aroused her from her reverie, she had only to look at them with her shining young eyes or to speak to them in her frank voice, and at once it was plain what endeared her to them all : her ready willingness, her upright nature, her perfect self-control, and her complete unselfishness. Whether Maguern said : ' Bring the soup,' or the burly Ange remarked : ' The soup's not salt enough,' or the sickly Alexis asked for ' three spoonfuls,' she did their bidding with the same quick willingness.

The Maguerns had long since adopted town customs : the men did not share a common soup bowl, but each had his plate that Anna filled. She, Denise, and even the mistress of the house ate when they could, standing up or sitting on one of the chests at the foot of the beds, which were of the ancient closed kind often surviving in Brittany.

For more than ten minutes nothing could be heard but the rattle of spoons and the banging down of tumblers. From outside, above the wind which whistled beneath the door, came the barking of Rabigo, the dog, who every night chased rabbits and martens and occasionally strayed as far as Penmur Pool for his hunting.

The three women were dressed nearly alike in shabby lace-trimmed black. They wore no caps, but their hair, plain in front, was plaited and caught in a net behind. On Sundays, however, even at a distance it could be seen that they came from two different parts of Brittany. Marie Maguern and Denise wore the traditional head-dress of the place : a strip of embroidered muslin that, hanging upon each side of the face, was bent at right angles on a level with the ears and fastened high up behind with a long pin. Anna wore a brown pad covered with embroidered lace set two or three inches above her forehead like a diadem. Several folds of muslin covered her massed fair hair.

Having eaten his share of the omelette and a good helping of salad, Jean-Guillaume got up, saying to Gildas :

' What did you do after the ploughing, while I was fetching the heifer ? '

' What you told me, father. I took the mare to the blacksmith's at Muzillac.'

' Did you ride ? '

' Yes. Bounce is a good trotter. The wind blew in her nostrils so hard that it made her sneeze.'

The children began to laugh.

' Don't laugh ! ' their father commanded. ' At your age, it's true, you can't be for ever thinking of the war, as we grown-ups are. We can't get it out of our minds, and I hate folks to laugh. Now, Gildas, did you hear any news in the town ? '

The young man slowly bent his right arm and fumbled in his jacket pocket.

' Your arm still bothers you ? '

' A bit. But that won't be for long. Coming home I used both hands, and I galloped on the Vannes road.'

As he spoke he unfolded the newspaper he had bought in Muzillac. The three women at once drew near to his corner of the table, Denise first and her mother-in-law close behind. Anna remained in the shadow : all that could be seen of her was her white forehead and her two fair locks.

' There's only this. It's the communiqué of December

20, 1915 : " A successful surprise attack, delivered at a salient of the German line in the neighbourhood of Loos . . ." '

' Dear God ! Pol might have been there ! '

Denise, her face grown white, leaned for support against the corner of the table.

' No, no, my girl,' Maguern said gently. ' Pol isn't in the Loos district. Loos is in Artois. . . . He's somewhere near Verdun.'

' They're fighting everywhere and the papers tell us so little . . .'

' Let Gildas go on ! '

' . . . " resulted in the bringing in of thirty-two prisoners and three machine-guns. Bad weather is general on all parts of the front. There is nothing further to report." '

Maguern looked towards the window rattling in the wind. Listening to the woodwork creaking in the storm, he said :

' When this wind gets there it's got no strength left, and the rain begins. Like the rest of us, it's had enough of battles. Wasn't it Orgebin wrote to the folk next door a day or two back that the men in the trenches were up to their knees in water ? '

' He said " up to their waists," Jean-Guillaume,' his wife interrupted.

' That's it—up to their waists. Some have been known to disappear in the sodden earth. The rain never stops. Or if it does, the snow begins, and the bullets fly overhead all the time. It's downright misery out there, children.'

The young folk looked at him as though he were telling a story and they were awaiting its end. They guessed the grief on the lowered faces of the grown-ups. Denise, unable to restrain her tears, withdrew to the far end of the room and sat on the chest at the foot of her closed box-bed. Maguern instinctively clasped his hands, resting them upon the table. The man's faith was a living thing, and sorrow sent him, as though under strong compulsion, instantly to prayer. Then he continued his story. He knew what had befallen neighbours of his. On the evening before, in talk by his shed with Trébestan, a crony of his and a retired army man, he had remarked : ' Even the young should be made to know the misery of our day. Then they will better be able to seek God's pardon. His forgiveness is not to be had at the first time of asking. Words don't win it. It's men's hearts God looks at.'

His children leaned towards Jean-Guillaume as he sat with tight clasped hands : ' According to the Orgebin boy the men were marching on a road full of shell-holes. The weather was as bad as it is to-night. Worse ; for the rain fell in buckets, and it was pitch-black. The men couldn't see their hands in front of their faces. A man marching beside Orgebin fell over on his face. Orgebin jumped to one side away from the shell-hole, shouting : " Stephen, where are you ? " The men behind stopped short. Stooping, Orgebin thought he could see a hand waving in the air, clutching a rifle, and he thought he heard somebody crying " Help ! " He groped about and tried to find the man. But Stephen Vandour was in his grave ; he had vanished, body, arm, rifle, and all, and all the rest could do was to tell their comrades behind not to fall into the hole. Of course there were plenty to offer a prayer for their neighbour as all good Christians should, and as we will do now.'

From near her bed Denise Maguern sobbed. None
turned at her sob. The children, their mother, the family
servant—all looked at Jean-Guillaume, who had raised
his head. In the lamplight which fell full upon him he
stood watching the storm-buffetted window opposite.
His usually firm lips were drooping at the corners. The
old man was near to tears, but he had great self-control.
He unclasped his hands, and fingered the small tufts of
white hair—his ' rabbit's paws ' as the children called
them—which grew upon his ears, as if they were flies
he wanted to brush off. He said :

' When Gildas goes, I hope the weather will be better.
I've seen my share of bad weather ; yes, I've seen my
share. It comes and it goes, nobody knows why. It's
God's will. Let us now pray for Stephen, young
Orgebin's comrade.'

He got up.

A moment later all were upon their knees on the hard
and uneven floor of the living-room, their faces turned
towards the hearth, where the dying coals were momentarily quickened by gusts of wind that drove down the
chimney, and to the crucifix which hung above the
mantel-shelf.

To-night Jean-Guillaume said prayers, and after them
a litany of the patron saints of all the family, including
his niece's. At the end he added : ' S. Stephen . . .'

' Pray for him ! ' they all responded.

He went on, as his habit was on solemn occasions :

' The forefathers of our family . . .'

' Pray for us ! '

' Saints of the Great War . . .'

' Pray for us ! '

' May God guard us all ! '

' Amen ! '

They rose from their knees. The boys made their
way to the room on the right, next to the stable. Denise
and Anna remained in the living-room, where each had
a curtained bed over a chest of waxed wood. The
husband and wife, opening the left-hand door, went into
the narrow low-pitched room, lit by a diminutive
window, which had been theirs since their eldest son's
marriage. The night had filled them with melancholy.
So it must have been in such farms as this in the time
of Joan of Arc, when fathers spoke to their children of
the pitiable state of the kingdom of France.

Jean-Guillaume lit the lantern which served them as
lamp. He had scarcely put it down upon the wooden
chest by the wall, when his wife said :

' Jean-Guillaume ! '

' What is it ? '

' Anna's not spoken to you ? '

' No.'

' She hasn't the courage. But she has to me. Her
father is coming here to-morrow morning.'

' To this house ? He'd better not, unless he's ready
to pay me the five thousand francs he owes me. Otherwise he'd better keep away.'

' You can't expect it. Your brother is worse off than
ever. Anna, poor girl, told me he had to sell one of his
black cows. She cried when she told me.'

' At that rate he has only two left. Take it from me,
before the year's out he'll have done with farming. It
would be hard enough for a good farmer to keep such a
place going. All his wheatland put together isn't much
bigger than a good-sized cabbage patch. And when
it comes to my brother with his fishing and poaching,

how can he expect to get a living out of a farm ? He'd better not come here, I tell you. . . .'

'Last time he didn't come in. But I'll tell Anna you don't wish it.'

Jean-Guillaume, his jacket already off, unbuttoned and removed his waistcoat, hanging it over a chair. His wife stood opposite to him, leaning against the wall, and made no move to undress. The light, protected though it was by its stout round lamp-glass, from time to time spurted and smoked. The howling of the wind became a long shriek.

'A storm over Brittany and rain for the men out there !' Maguern exclaimed. 'Why aren't you undressing, Marie ? '

She had been looking towards the dormer window at which the whistling wind drove wildly. Turning her head, she answered :

'It's like this, Jean-Guillaume. I've left a pair of sheets out from the washing on the moor. They weren't quite dry. I've weighted down the corners, and I know the wind won't carry them off. . . .'

'Who should, then ? Why worry about them ? You can get them in the morning.'

Still his wife made no move. Jean-Guillaume shrugged his shoulders, and in a hard voice said :

'I see what it is. You're afraid my brother Corentin will go that way before you to-morrow morning. Stop worrying. It's time we went to sleep.'

His wife began to take off her clothes. Within a few minutes all at Penmur farm were sleeping. Outside the storm drove the spray a hundred yards inland, and on the uplands it bent the gnarled pines whose roots, spreading in ridges, here gripped the pebbles, there clung to the furze and the broom, and in this borrowed strength held fast.

Disturbed at the news she had heard, Pol Maguern's wife woke at intervals. Her thoughts were with the men at the front. Finally, after an hour of restlessness in which nightmare alternated with prayer, the young wife fell asleep.

Anna thought of the morrow. She saw her father arrive in the cart of a friend or of some good-natured stranger met upon the road. She saw him walking with her round the farm whose house he must not enter. She remembered too that Christmas was very near and that for Christmas she had arranged a surprise, something in which she would look lovelier than any girl in Muzillac, in Ambon, or in Billiers. None knew of her folly. Gildas was as ignorant as the rest. Yet it was for Gildas and for Gildas alone that she had gone to the shop with all her savings.

The small parcel, still wrapped in its tissue paper and tied with its red ribbon, was in the chest of her box-bed. Earlier in the evening, when the living-room had been empty, she had unfolded her apron, which was of such expensive material that not even the rich farmers' daughters had dared to buy it, though two of them had bargained for it. Yet the expense was of no account if Gildas thought her beautiful in it, and if, thinking her beautiful, he uttered words of love that he had not yet uttered. For her part she loved him dearly. Although this was a secret, it was but half a secret. He must surely know that she thought only of him. That night of all the Penmur household she alone slept with a smile on her lips.

The storm could not touch her.

CHAPTER II

THE HOUSEHOLD OF THE ISLES

Soon after daybreak Jean-Guillaume said to his wife :

' Don't go to get your sheets this morning : leave it till my brother has gone again.'

He went into the next room. Pol's wife and the servant were already at work in their clattering clogs. Maguern said to Anna :

' Take the beasts when you go. Take them to the moor down yonder. Look after them just as you did when you were a little girl. There's no need to be back before twelve or thereabouts.'

Gathering from this that she was free to see her father on the moor, Anna led out the cattle. There were a dozen of them in all, bullocks, cows and yearlings, all Nantes stock. Their light hides distinguished them from the black-and-white Breton animals.

Putting on her warm black frock with an apron of thick grey wool, she took a switch from the farmyard and opened the stable door. She went from beast to beast, allowing their loosened ropes and chains to fall with a clatter to the ground. She chanted their names, which she knew as well as her prayers, so that each animal might know her to have charge of him that day. Beginning her cow-herd's duties, she followed the cattle as they straggled through the farmyard, making for the trees and shrubs that bounded it. On the short grassland of the plateau, one of the highest points of that country-side, she allowed them to stray where they would. The soil was poor : low, scattered clumps of furze and heath made so many small islands in a green sea of grass.

At that hour—eight o'clock in the morning—no one was to be seen. Beneath the clear sky, swept clean of clouds by last night's wind, cold breezes still scurried— rearguards of the storm which they sought to overtake. Anna chose one of the many granite blocks which were scattered over the moor and sat down. With Rabigo at her feet, she began to knit.

The men—Gildas, Ange and their father—had taken the track which skirted the farm on its lower side and for rather more than a hundred yards followed the cliff with its double slope. Leaving this, it branched into the best land of Penmur farm, whose deep soil, reddish brown verging on black, was rich with broken and disintegrating roots and with all the silt of the ancient tillages.

It was here that the men had begun to work. Maguern drove the plough. Behind him with a heavy spade Ange broke up the clods left in the furrow, using now the edge and now the flat of the blade ; in front, Gildas led the two oxen. For Jean-Guillaume with his customary thrift had judged two to be sufficient to work the light soil of Four Days Field.

The team went at its usual plodding pace. From time to time the voice of the goadsman calling the names of the oxen reached the moor : ' Bileux ! Major !—Major ! Bileux ! ' The shout was clearest at the end of the

furrows when the team had to turn either left or right :
' Hoo-Hup ! Bileux ! . . . Ock-la, Major ! ' On the
moor above Anna, lost in dreams, at each cry moved
her lips as though they would kiss the wind which
carried it. Whether she were happy or unhappy she
was not sure. She was waiting for her father.

She had not long to wait. He came without a sound.
Rabigo, full length on the grass with his nose on his
outstretched paws, opened his pink eyes, but had no
time to bark before Corentin Maguern stood over them.
From behind Anna he said :

' Good morning, my girl ! '

With the free swift movement of youth she stood upon
her feet, making no pause in her knitting. As she turned
to kiss her father, her needles ceased to click ; a moment
later they clicked again. Corentin Maguern took her
into his arms and kissed her on both cheeks. He
kissed her so for two reasons. In the first place he
loved his child Anna. In the second, he was proud
of the girl who in her comely Breton womanhood
seemed to him, had he expressed his thoughts, to be
kin to the saints of the Calvary in the Forest of
Fouesnant.

' Good morning, father. You said in your letter you
would be here before twelve, but I didn't expect you as
soon as this.'

The man took a step or two backward that he might
see her better. The racing clouds scurried on.

' Surely you know, Anna, that I'm not the kind of
man who keeps to time-table. I have to come and go
when I can. I ran across the egg merchant from Surzur.
He gave me a lift in his car and dropped me and the
bicycle half a mile away. And here I am ! '

Anna, looking in the direction from which her father had come, saw his bicycle leaning on a clump of broom.

They sat down to talk within a few paces of each other. Their seats were the broken weather-worn rocks, centuries old, which crop through the soil in that part of the country. Before he took his seat, Corentin Maguern turned towards his brother's farm, half hidden from where he stood—his brother's farm that he was forbidden to enter.

' They're all keeping well over there ? '

' Yes, they all keep well.'

' Denise hasn't had her baby yet ? '

' No. She expects it at the end of March or thereabouts.'

' Three months yet. In war-time that's a long time.'

' What do you mean, father ? '

' Mean ? Nothing. And who's to bring up this child ? You, I suppose—as usual ! '

' Maybe.'

' Say surely ! Its mother hasn't much go. My sister-in-law is getting old. It will all fall on you—as usual. Feeding-bottles to get ready, napkins to wash, rocking the cradle, driving away the flies in the day-time, and watching the little brat at night when it cries for nothing. It all falls on the servant—I've told you that before.'

She put the ball of wool upon her lap, then the knitting and the needles. She sat very still. Her fine face had set in strangely firm lines. Her youth seemed to have fled. Sudden stubbornness showed itself when she spoke ; her tones were as stubborn as her words. As stubborn were her eyes, gazing straight and wide before her.

' If I like to work, that's my affair.'

The words were more than an expression of willingness. They were both a reproach and a secret defiance. The man understood. There on the moor they sat, and for a long moment the silence between them was unbroken. Each looked at the other : the girl sat erect ; the man bent forward, his elbows on his knees, his holly stick in his hands.

He was handsome in a fashion, taller than his younger brother, with a cadaverous expression. His strong frame looked wasted. In complexion he was brown with a tinge of green in the brown : a man with water-fowl colouring, he might have been called ! Like his brother, he wore a felt hat with up-turned brim and velvet braid. Like his brother's, his jacket was short, with horn buttons; his trousers were too short and showed his shabby half-boots. These trousers were of a durable blue-and-white striped cloth, a material never found outside Brittany.

The general cast of Corentin's features hinted at Chouan forbears. There was about him a suggestion of mixed pugnacity and shiftlessness. His bright, restless, twinkling eyes indicated that here was a man capable of cunning but not of fear. He had the temperament of an artist, a dreamer, a born musician. Yet none had heard Corentin Maguern sing a catch of his own composition, as none had seen him set fingers on the keys of an accordion.

When he perceived his daughter's unspoken condemnation, his mind went swiftly to this thought and that. Various courses were open to him : he might defend himself ; he might attempt some explanation ; he might resort to anger or a show of it. Unwilling that she should know how much her words had hurt him, he was content to let the moments go by in silence. In their grazing the cattle had scattered : his eyes watched them idly as he said :

'You'd have less work to do at my place, Anna.'

Then remembering how large a part conscience played with her, he added :

'Besides, you'll be doing your duty, if you come home.'

The girl shook her head, but did not lift her eyes from the knitting which she had meanwhile resumed. At that moment, the moorland wind bore from the distant meadow the shouted encouragement to the ploughing oxen : 'Ock-la, Major ! . . .' Anna shook her head still more vigorously.

'You're a woman now '—he meant that she was of age—' or I should have the right to order you home. But now you're no longer bound to do as I say. You're a law to yourself. Still, you've a good heart ; so you'll take pity on your old father, won't you ? Look here ! I've a bit of news for you from your old home—your own home ; not this place, but the place where you were born and grew up. Well, just now there's no one at home except me. I'm alone.'

Anna raised her eyes. She showed no less animation than he, when she asked :

'What about the boys ? '

Corentin Maguern's railing laughter echoed among the broom bushes :

'The boys ? So you've forgotten your elder brother started his training this year ? He had to report at Brest recruiting station : they've put him in the blue-jacket training school. Soon he'll be doing his bit for France on board ship.'

' And the little one ? '

' The little one ! I like that—he's taller than you ! I've got no hold on him. He's a chip of the old block, he is. He'll take anything except orders. He's gone too!'

' Gone ! Where ? '

' To sea, of course ! Where else would he go from a place like ours ? Our land won't hold you down. One fine morning he came along to tell me that he had signed on a Bourgneuf trawler. It's a deep-sea boat in the ordinary way, but since the war they've turned deep-sea trawlers into mine-sweepers. So it comes to this : I'm alone ! '

' Poor father ! '

Anna's face had softened. Under their peaceful brows her tranquil eyes watched the varying expressions which played over her father's features. When he had said ' I'm alone ! ' he had laughed. In his laughter there had been both anger and irony. Then the anger died ; the irony was lost in sudden gentleness. Memory of happier days, recollection of sorrows as hidden as they were deep, momentarily put from him his normal mood of railing resolution. Yet his next gesture scarcely fitted this gentler mood ; for with his right hand he raised his holly stick, plunging it with such violence into the earth that the ferrule and several inches of wood disappeared into the loose top-soil of the moor, while the stick itself stood quivering as if the sap still ran in it. For a second time he said :

' Alone ! '

The reflection may have crossed his mind that like his stick he had neither root nor branch. When after a pause he spoke again, it was as if in thought he had come back from far wandering :

' Five years ago when you left home, your mother was still alive. . . . Since she died, I've tried to run the house as well as do the work of the farm. The boys helped me. The work's been done after a style, though the good kind neighbours jeered at us for doing it. Just now there's a woman from the Island comes in to make my bed and to put the place straight. . . .'

The discordant cackle of his laughter was not good to hear. Momentarily it lifted the corners of his mouth and left deep hollows in his cheeks.

' You're no fool, Anna : no need for me to tell you what sort of woman'll come in to char three hours in the morning and two in the afternoon for a man like me who hasn't a soul ! '

The words grieved Anna. Because of her grief, with an unobtrusive thumb she made the sign of the cross above her heart. Seeing this, he went on :

' So there's no two ways about it : you'll have to come back.'

Her answer was swift and unhesitating :

' No, father. My place is here.'

From Four Days Field came the cry to the oxen :

' Ock-la, Major ! '

Leaning both hands on his stick, with a thrust of his loins the man got upon his feet. His daughter stood also. From his greater height he looked down upon her, his face clouded and strange with his discontent. The moor stretched lonely around them as they stood apart.

' Going, father ? '

' Don't be in such a hurry, my girl ! If I'm going to let you stay here, you'll have to get hold of some money for me.'

Anna turned pale. Once more the voice of Gildas came floating on the keen air of the moor.

'I'll wait here for you,' her father said. 'Run along with you! You make a pretty penny over there . . . !'

'Not so much as you'd think. And I've had to spend a good bit, what's more.'

'On your back, I suppose ? '

'It looks like it, doesn't it ? '

'What about me then, if it comes to that ? Except for my breeches every stitch I'm wearing is ten years old, Good Lord, girl! by rights I should be getting a pension from you. It's damnable. Even your brothers send me what they can. Run along with you! Look in your bottom drawer behind your head-dresses! Or better still, get some from my brother. He owes it you, and I want it. What's more, I mean to have it. If I don't get it, there's going to be a row.'

As if to ward off his threat, the girl put her hands before her face. Walking quickly, she covered the fifty yards of intervening moorland and gained the oaks and furze which ringed the hidden farm. Taking the sunken road which led down to it, she reached the farmyard and entered the house. On her return ten minutes later she saw that the bicycle was no longer lying on the grass. Probably (she thought) her father had wheeled the machine out of reach of the cattle ; perhaps he had leaned it against the tall bushes dividing the moor from a newly sown field on the plateau. In any case Corentin Maguern himself had come back and was at the place where they had talked before.

The packet, wrapped in a piece of grey woollen cloth and tied with pack-thread, which Anna carried in her right hand, contained five- and ten-franc notes together with small change in coppers.

'There's a hundred and fifty-one francs in there,' she said. 'That's everything I've got.'

Corentin held out his hand :

'So you've been spending your money on somebody, have you ? Who is it ? ' he asked her. He stuffed the notes into his jacket pocket : with deliberate fingers he pressed them down three times as he was in the habit of doing with the wad of his shot-gun.

'The same old story ! You're all alike. You all treat your poor old father the same way. Still—thanks, thanks ! '

Hooking his holly stick over his right wrist, he stared at his daughter's face, to which agitation and her quick walking had brought a flush. His stare told him nothing : he could not guess upon whom she spent her savings. For Anna, as completely mistress of her eyes as of her lips, was as unmoved beneath his scrutiny as is a wall beneath the glare of the sun.

' Hoo-Hup ! Bileux ! '

Once again the faint cry came over the moor. The very broom bushes were not more impassive than Anna. Corentin broke into laughter—an old device of his when he wished to rid himself of embarrassment. Drawing his daughter to him, he kissed her good-bye.

' My word, Anna, you're a beauty ! If any time you think of marrying the captain of a coaster or the skipper of a deep-sea boat—it makes no odds—all you need do is to come back home. One of 'em is sure to be mooning about. Good-bye for a bit. When I'm broke, you'll see me again.'

Whirling his stick, with quick strides he began to

follow the track which men and cattle had trodden across the moor. He was soon out of sight. Anna went her way towards the farm. At the point where the trees and circling thicket raised their protecting barricade about the house, she noticed that the pair of sheets left by her aunt were no longer stretched over the bushes. She had no sooner set foot in the farmyard when her mistress called out :

' Did you fold up my sheets, Anna ? '

' No, aunt.'

' They were on the bushes half an hour ago. I sent Armandine out to look. Where are they now ? I should have told her to bring them, instead of trying to do everything myself. Where are they, I want to know ? '

With an expressive gesture she threw out her arms. As she had no wish to say what was in her mind, she hurried in the direction of the chicken-house. There were others, however, who had heard what she had said and who guessed what she had left unsaid. The eleven-year-old Armandine, hearing her name, came to the front door and saw Anna approaching. Turning to her mother, she said, fingering the corner of her apron :

' No need to look far, I should think, if you want to find the sheets. . . .'

It was her father and not her mother who answered. Home from ploughing, he had come into the farmyard ahead of his team and in front of Gildas and Ange. He looked up. So that none should miss his meaning, he raised his voice to growl :

' You mustn't say that, Armandine. It's better not to look for them. It's war-time. Things are bad. If we found they'd been stolen, somebody's reputation would suffer.'

At the end of the farmyard his wife, less tolerant than himself, set her shoulders angrily as she opened the door of the chicken-house. Armandine continued to mutter and as Gildas and Ange, now close to the stable door, might overhear her muttering, Maguern began again in the same loud voice :

' Listen to me, Armandine ! I haven't always money to give away. But if I choose to make a present of my sheets, nobody here has the right to pass remarks.'

He began to unyoke the beasts. At his side Gildas, who had heard something but not all, asked :

' What was she saying ? '

' Nothing, my boy, nothing ! That's all a chattering female ever does say.'

Dinner, a silent and melancholy meal, was soon over. The only remark was made by the ailing Alexis, as they were finishing.

' It's Christmas Eve to-morrow,' he said. ' Mother's promised to take me to Midnight Mass.'

At once there was a babel of voices. The two youngest children were eager to make this night excursion to Muzillac, while their parents pretended a reluctance to take them. Their joy was uproarious when finally consent was given. It was agreed that the whole party should go in the waggonette. They were to start at the first pealing of the church bells. Denise and Anna were to stay and look after the house.

CHAPTER III

A TALK ON THE MOOR

THE following evening, as the first peal of the bells came on the cold night air, they crowded into the waggonette drawn up in the middle of the yard. Lighting the lantern and drawing tight the mare's bridle rein, Gildas said : ' I'm going on my bicycle ; I shall be there almost as soon as you.' He said ' almost ' for he knew that, with a good meal inside her and with his father's ready whip to help her on, Bounce would be in fine fettle. All was ready. The mare was restless at the delay, and in her impatience began to back.

' Let her go, Gildas,' Jean-Guillaume shouted.

With flanks jog-jogging in the shafts and to the sound of slapping reins, Bounce, jolting over loose stones and splashing through farmyard slush, climbed the sloping yard. To cries of alarm from the children and their mother, she reached the moor and disappeared beyond the bushes. Once she got to the upland road, however, her steady gallop assured them of her good temper. In that sleeping country-side the clatter of her iron shoes over scattered flints was like the clanging of hammers ; the crunching of the wheels like the whirring of a grindstone.

Meanwhile Gildas had started. Wheeling his bicycle, he too climbed the slope between farm and moor. He

picked his way through the shadowy coppice and came
out upon the windy crest where, as he termed it, the
' good road ' began. From the shadow of the wood a
smaller shadow detached itself : a young woman
approached. It was Anna. This trysting-place had been
arranged between them to give her the opportunity of a
talk with him before he went to the war. On the green
verge the two walked along together, Gildas wheeling
his bicycle. The moon, three days from the full, made the
night like a diminished day. Every twig, every leaf, had
its well-defined shadow. In the still cold air no grass-
blade stirred. The light breeze which delicately skimmed
the earth caught as in a net multitudinous white specks
that were either dust or snow.

Anna was still in her working clothes. To avoid her
companion's gaze she stared straight at the fields before
them. She began :

' I can't think of anything, Gildas, except that you're
going to the war.'

' Yes, only nine days now ! I've got to go up on the
third of January. If I hadn't broken my arm, I should
have gone long enough ago.'

' Gildas—you were not fifteen when I first came to the
farm. Now you're a man. How much do you care for
me, Gildas . . .'

Without halting, he turned slightly towards her as
he said :

' You're a very dear friend.'

' It's true enough nobody's been as kind to me as you ;
but, you see, father wants me home again.'

Gildas stopped and took her hand.

' Don't go—don't leave us, Anna ! '

' But you're leaving us, anyway.'

She walked on. Still avoiding his face, she kept her gaze so steadfast before her that she might have been reading the questions which she put to him. She was in fact reading them—she was reading them from her soul.

' Tell me, Gildas ! If God brings you back safe and sound, are we going to be married ? Is that why you say " Don't go ! " ? Do you care enough ? '

' Sometimes I think so.'

At this answer she trembled in all her limbs. In the moonlight they walked on a few more steps, their breathing the only sound between them. The moor stretching some way ahead was bathed in moonlight. For the first time that evening Anna turned towards Gildas, and he saw surpassing happiness upon a girl's face.

' When you come back to Penmur,' she continued, ' if I'm still there, you won't be able to bring the tailor— you can't, if we both live at the same place.'

(She alluded to the old custom : a young man will take a friend with him—the friend is in fact the *kemener*, or wedding tailor—to visit the girl's parents, revealing this ' friend's ' identity only at the end of the visit.)

There was tenderness in their laughter.

' But, Gildas, I'm older than you ! '

' Only two years—what does that matter ? '

' Father's poor, you know.'

Gildas made an impatient gesture, no doubt to dismiss the thought of his uncle. He came of an old Breton family. The bare idea that he could be suspected of trifling with Anna wounded him to the quick. For his sincerity was innate. Apart from the sudden gravity of his face, that gesture was his only answer. Reaching the hedge of young gorse bushes between the

moor and the road, they stood in clear straight silhouette,
their shadows in the moonlight making a single shadow
behind them.

The pair stopped short. In silent agreement they
turned towards Penmur farm, whose roofs were seen as a
black smudge at the foot of the hill. They talked in low
tones, fearing that the very wind would hear them and
tell their secret.

' You know I'm fond of you, Anna—I've not tried to
hide it enough.'

' You've tried too hard, always.'

' But I didn't mean to tell you. I vowed I'd go
without telling you. I may be killed.'

' No, you won't—you wont.'

' Wounded maybe; three Muzillac men have been
already. I mayn't be able to work any more.'

' No, you won't be wounded. My prayers'll keep you
safe. You'll come back just the same. You'll be fonder
of me, that's all.'

' Fonder—why ? '

' Because you won't have seen me for all that time.'

Sudden shyness made them look away from each other.
He was the more self-possessed, and spoke first after a
brief moment of silent delight against which he struggled.

' Besides, Anna . . .'

' Oh, so there's something else, is there ? I've been
afraid there was ! '

He bent over his handle-bars the better to hide
his face.

' It was . . . before I met you, Anna . . . a long
time before . . . I wanted——'

' Who ? A girl from Muzillac ? '

' No.'

' From Ambon then, or Damgan ? '

' No.'

' From Billiers or some other place ? '

' No ! '

' Well, you can have her, whoever she is ! You like her more than you do me. I shan't stand in your way ! '

She said this so fiercely and in so clear a voice that any passer must have overheard her. At that late hour, however, the road was deserted. Gildas Maguern stiffened. His hands trembled as he turned his machine towards the highway. Anna could see his face white under the moon and his eyes poignant with the effort it cost him to speak.

' No, it isn't that—it's something else. I'm sure I'm not doing wrong in loving you, Anna, but even when I am loving you, I sometimes think of it. Time and time again it has tormented me. I haven't told a soul . . . I can't tell you any more—not now. It's madness— I've told myself that. Perhaps it'll go as it came, and then—— Oh, Anna ! Anna !—Well, good-bye—good-bye ! '

He mounted his bicycle and rode away. As a ship over the horizon he passed over the crest and disappeared. Anna watched his lengthening shadow till shadow and man were gone.

With slow steps and hands crossed as if in prayer Anna returned over the moonlit moor. Because of her tears she no longer saw the path, but stumbled through the young gorse bushes and cut stumps of last year's growth. What was it he had begun to tell her—had begun and then had stopped ? He who spoke so little had spoken at last, only to deny something of which she had been quite sure. She had felt his agony : five years of life under the same roof with Gildas had taught her much of the man. There had been many small signs of his preference for her and of his happiness in her company : such trifles as a smile when he met her and the warmth of his greeting. Then there were presents from the fair . . . there was his constant eagerness to help her. . . .

With twitching lips she half murmured, half moaned : ' Only yesterday Aunt Marie told me to draw three buckets of water for the sick beasts. He got to the well in front of me—it's a queer noise that well makes when the handle's turned : " Hi-ha-hi " it seems to say— and drew the three buckets while I stood and listened. I beat time to it and Gildas laughed at me. His laughter meant : " I wouldn't do this for anyone else, only for Anna, my cousin, my dear." And when a man laughs like that and looks into a girl's eyes for his thanks— especially when he's no scamp but an honest man like Gildas, then he must care and must be waiting till he is old enough to say . . . what he didn't say. Oh, it was hard for him to answer ! He's not the deceiving sort. What is the trouble ? It can only be a girl he was fond of when he was a youngster—before he knew me. And he doesn't know how to get out of it. It seems she doesn't come from Muzillac or from Damgan or from Billiers—in fact, it's sure she doesn't : he said so. Perhaps she's from Vannes or from S. Anne : he always remembers her feast on the twenty-sixth of July. Poor Gildas ! It's plain he's worried and wants to be free— free to marry me. Surely I can't be loving a man who loves somebody else. I can't be mistaken : I've seen him every day for all this time. I know he loves me, yet doesn't like to tell me so. . . . But he will ! . . . He may even tell me to-morrow when we're coming back from Muzillac, and when just to please him I've got on my . . .'

Beginning to walk down the hill towards the farm, she stopped in the shadow of the trees to look at the dark outline of the house. Only one window—Denise's room —showed a light. Then she smiled, as she remembered that the morrow was Christmas Day. What a Christmas Day that would be, if he came home from Mass with her dressed in her best, dressed better than any girl in Muzillac, even the richest ! Oh, it was a mad thing that she had done ! All her savings for a year or more gone at once ! Yet if he were pleased, and proud of her, it was worth it ! To-morrow ! To-morrow !

Once more she grew thoughtful. Perhaps it wasn't a woman. If it weren't, what was it ? Perhaps it was town-life that attracted him as it did so many. Or the sea, maybe. Bretons are born sailors : they'd go to the ends of the earth in their boats. She shook her small shapely head in dismissal of these thoughts. Within her own recollection several Maguerns had gone to sea, and in each case there had been a sufficient reason, whether it were a father's misfortune or persuasion of the mother's blood—particularly when the mother came from her own sea-loving Arzon folk. But with Gildas it was the soil and not the sea which called. Hunger for adventure had not been his. Essentially he was a goadsman, a drover, a cheerful ploughman who encouraged his beasts, as only that morning (Anna reflected) he had done over there, past those black roofs, in Four Days Field.

No, he was afraid he'd be killed, and so bring grief on his sweetheart—that must be the trouble . . . but

to-morrow—to-morrow ! . . . on the way back from
Muzillac . . . if only it would keep fine !

Anna went into the farmyard, empty save for a cat
that picked its way from stone to stone to avoid the
slush. She looked anxiously at the sky, first to the
south over Penmur Pool ; then to the west whence the
clouds were driving. All was still : at intervals a faint
mist hid the stars. It was cold—but she did not notice
this. Softly she opened the door of the room where
Denise was sleeping. The night-light flickered in the
draught from the chimney. Undressing quickly she said
her prayers with more than her usual fervour, and drew
the curtains of her box-bed. The valances, however,
did not meet, and through the small chink she would be
able to see Jean-Guillaume, Gildas, Alexis, Armandine,
and their mother when they came back from Midnight
Mass. . . .

It was over two hours before the dog gave the first
warning of their return. Though the road was some
distance away, the wild Rabigo with his quick ear heard
the wheels of the Penmur waggonette and the trotting
of the mare, his friend in the farmyard, as no doubt he
would have done among a dozen others. Pol's wife slept,
and only Anna heard him as he ran barking first to the
bottom of the yard and then out upon the hill. For ten
minutes there was no sound ; the waggonette must have
turned sharply, leaving the road for the narrow path
which forced the mare to a walk. Then young voices
could be heard in the yard.

' It was good, wasn't it, Armandine ? '

' Yes, I liked the anthem best.'

' Which ? '

' " The angels in the fields sang joyfully." '

She sang a few bars of the hymn. Her pure young treble rose and fell on the night air.

' Be quiet, Armandine ! They're asleep indoors.'

Their father's gruff voice put an abrupt end to the girl's singing. Anna heard them laughing, and after the laughter the clanking of the bit as Jean-Guillaume exchanged the mare's bridle for her halter.

As the living-room door was opened quietly, another and stronger voice began upon a second air that was not a Christmas tune.

' Quiet, children—quiet ! You'll wake Denise and Anna.'

The five of them who had been to Mass came into the living-room in a body. Each took a glass of cider and a piece of bread from the table and went away eating, the parents to their room on the left, the boys to theirs on the right. Armandine, left alone, did not take long to undress and go to bed.

All Anna's attention had been for Gildas, who had gone out with the others. Kneeling on her bed and holding her breath, she peered intently through the curtain as she watched him where he stood by his brothers Alexis and Ange ; now talking to his father ; now cautiously touching glasses to follow the custom, and now discussing the next day's work which must be started in a few hours.

' As you like, father. I'll stay or I'll go.'

The old man considered for a moment. Anna grew cold : if Gildas did not go to High Mass at Muzillac, her ' surprise ' would fall flat and all hope be lost. As Anna knew, it was Jean-Guillaume's habit after his first communion to attend second Mass. As he considered, his white whiskers showing against his full red face, he looked (Anna thought) rather like a judge. She had seen that same expression many times before, when some decision had to be reached which affected the farm. It was such a decision that Gildas now gravely awaited, and that he would carry out unquestioningly. Upon this, too, Anna's plans, that none suspected unless it were Gildas, now depended.

Jean-Guillaume raised his glass again, took two gulps of cider and set down the glass.

' You'd better harness Bounce,' he said finally. ' She goes faster than Nigger, but your wrist is quite well now. You go, my boy ! Once you're at the war, you won't get the chance. Perhaps this is the last time you'll go to our church till it's over.'

' All right, father. I'll get her ready.'

The curtains of the box-bed shook a little as Anna craned forward. Had Gildas looked towards that end of the room, he would have seen two eyes shining there in the shadow. Her first distress had changed to exultant gladness now that she knew Gildas was to go to Muzillac.

If the boy was pleased, he did not show it. Already he saw himself at the front. On the wall his fine proud profile was silhouetted in the faint lamp-light. Had he been in fact at the front, he would have looked much as he now looked. As their thoughts turned to the trenches, both father and son grew silent. Gildas gave a slight shudder as men do when they dream and awake from their dream. He too finished his cider. Putting down his glass, he went by the three curtained beds, Denise's, Anna's, and Armandine's. At the closed hangings of these he gave a single shy glance as he passed. Taking his youngest brother's hand, he followed Ange to the boy's room. Jean-Guillaume went into his own room, where the small Armandine had been getting ready for bed. In her night-gown, her feet bare and her hair in plaits, she climbed into the third and oldest of the box-beds next to Anna's.

From the still country without no sound came on this quiet Christmas morning. Flapping their wings and uttering mournful cries at the sight of the moonlit sparkle of Penmur Pool between its rushes, a flock of birds flew high over the house. The pool with its sparkle did not stay their flight. For the spell of the sea, which they saw afar off, was upon them. Their cries, wistful or desirous, grew more and more faint. The dog no longer barked ; the wind was no more than a piping—such a piping as a cricket makes in the hearth on a summer's evening.

CHAPTER IV

THE VELVET APRON

CHRISTMAS morning of 1915 was a morning of rich glowing light. Every grass-blade, every shoot and every bud was lovely with the ephemeral beauty of sparkling dewdrops. As on a summer's day the earth was a patchwork of sunshine and shadow. No wind stirred. Away at Billiers the sea had the smoothness of a mill-pond : if any Billiers fisherman had had the inclination to get out his boat—no likely thing on Christmas Day—he would certainly have stowed away his sou'wester.

Gildas fed the cattle with the aid of Ange, then went to change for High Mass. On his unmade bed in the boys' room he had laid out his best suit : trousers, waistcoat, and jacket, after the modern town style, which the tailor who supplied the well-to-do of Muzillac had made him less than two years before. It was almost half-past nine when, wearing his felt hat, he passed through the living-room on his way to harness Bounce.

Within a few minutes his mother was seated in the waggonette. Her bulk was at all times considerable, but now her billowing Sunday clothes scarcely left room for Armandine to squeeze in on her right. Gildas, reins in hand, cracked his whip repeatedly as a signal to Anna,

whose dressing had never before been so lengthy an
affair. Taking his watch from his waistcoat pocket, he
called :

'Anna ! Hurry up ! We're all waiting.'

Allowing Bounce, whose impatience exceeded his own,
to trot a few steps, Gildas drew her up opposite the front
door within two paces of the threshold. He bent to see
whether Anna at last were ready.

He straightened almost at once.

'You must look grand to-day, Anna,' he said, 'if
you've put your cloak on.'

Suppressed laughter came from behind him. To
Armandine the 'surprise' was no secret. On the doorstep Anna stood wrapped in a long black cloak—a
costume still worn in several Breton cantons by women
in mourning. Heavy and voluminous, it had been
given her by a relative living in S. Gildas. Anna had
sewn three clasps upon it, one at the neck, one at the
waist and one at the hem, to cover her dress completely.

'Hurry up and get in ! '

She walked round the waggonette and proudly took
her seat beside Gildas, drawing her cloak tightly round
her.

'Now then, Bounce ! '

The mare had done much heavy work for Maguern
and for his neighbours at the front. Yet she trotted
briskly out of the yard and, picking her way over the
many stones and the new shoots of furze and broom,
took the track across the moor. At the corner she broke
into a canter upon the road. Anna, sitting very erect,
did not speak. She folded her hands upon her missal to
keep it steady on her lap. Gildas turned to look at her
as they rounded the corner. On Anna's face was the

faint smile of one who anticipates delight at telling a secret.

' When you were doing up your cloak, I caught sight of something red. What was it, Anna ? ' Gildas asked.

' You'll see when we come out after Mass.'

' Everyone will see then.'

' Yes—they'll all see.'

' Then it's not for me that you've put on your fine clothes ? '

Very slightly she turned her head. Her glowing face and shining eyes said more eloquently than any words : ' It's for you (and you know it) that I've tried to make myself beautiful ; it's for you that I've spent my money. I would have you cherish the memory of Anna more beautifully dressed than usual. It is you—you who are about to go to the war—it is only you I love.'

He understood. He glanced significantly at the girl's cloak and at her crimped hair.

' From what I can see of it, it's not only your dress. Everything about you's looking very gay.'

' I'm not feeling very gay, Gildas.'

' Not feeling gay ! And it's Christmas morning ! '

' I know it's Christmas morning. It's also the Christmas before you go away.'

They said no more. As they drove, the air blew sweet in their faces. Till the first houses of Muzillac came in sight, for them the horizon had a dreaming beauty.

Bounce, made comfortable in a woollen rug with two straps, was stabled at an inn in the lower part of the town near the Nantes-Vannes road. Losing no time, the Maguerns climbed the steep Bourg-Paul at whose top stands the old church among still older houses. They skirted the Market Square and after ten minutes' brisk walking reached a smaller square which in the afternoons was entirely shadowed by the walls and roof of the church.

Afraid that they would be late, they walked as fast as they could, but Anna's new high-heeled shoes made her slower than usual. She still clasped her cloak tightly around her, but as they passed the Rose Inn a gust of wind blew up the hem and showed a glimpse of red beneath. One of the three Muzillac girls idling there cried after her : ' There's a humbug for you ! She's got new clothes on and doesn't want them seen. She's going to meet her boy at church ! ' Anna, struggling after Armandine and her mother, heard their pealing laughter behind her. Gildas with his long strides had outstripped the three of them some time before. He reached the church when the Gospel had scarcely begun, they when it was near its end. They seated themselves in the Penmur pew on the left of the nave. To the right of them Gildas had found a place with the men in the transept.

The church was crowded. On both sides of the nave the head-dresses of the women had the effect of massed white flowers. The altar was decked out for the festival. The preacher for Christmas Day left the Sanctuary : as he climbed the pulpit-stairs, the harmonium again played the Shepherds' Song :

> ' The heavenly Child is born to-day.
> String the lutes, the hautbois sound ! '

The children's faces shone ; their lips faintly murmured the words of the hymn. From their expressions, both young and old equally rejoiced at the thought of Christ's Nativity. The glances of many, straying towards the Tabernacle, were a witness to earth's oldest and supremest love. In that church were flesh and blood saints whose statues in marble the world would never see.

The priest stood silent for a moment in the pulpit. A man of about fifty, he came from Vannes, probably from one of the Orders there. The energy of his features contrasted with the calm of his bearing. As he stood there above the upturned faces of the congregation he was about to address, the obvious detachment of his spirit from earthly things was the man's chief characteristic. Throughout France he had preached to many and various congregations ; as priest, he had come into contact with many and diverse souls and for long had known both the beauty and the misery to be found in this world.

He had put illusion from him. He had grown accustomed to ingratitude. He was acquainted with man's many faults. He had seen repentance slide into retrogression. He had watched good resolutions first falter and then fail. Yet through it all he had kept his faith. For God whom he served had given him strength, while among his fellow-men certain saintly souls had brought him inspiration. One glance showed that this man could be deceived by neither lies nor flattery nor fine words, and made it plain that both fear and venality were unknown to him. Clearly his spiritual battle was already won, and the scars of that battle could not hide his deep inner peace.

He began to speak. His subject was the Nativity. His words were free from verbal prettiness, rhetorical eloquence, and purely literary ornament. He compared what we call our ' sacrifices ' with the love and supreme sacrifice of the Son of God who left his Father's heaven to become flesh, to suffer and to die in order to save men from damnation.

' He made that vast journey ; he forsook that excelling happiness ; he chose to undergo those great sufferings, knowing that his only reward would be insult and outrage. This happened once—it cannot happen again. Think on this. Each of you has been called—or is about to be called—to prove his courage. These days are man's great testing time. In every household familiar faces are missing ; no family can be gathered together under one roof. Often our dead themselves are lost to us ; for often the authorities can find no trace of them. Separation follows separation, and is there any shall dare to say who in this life will meet again ? Life will still be theirs, but whether, as our tender love would have them, on this earth—who shall say ? Let us not be niggard for France in our prayers ! There has never been a time when our soul's enemy has not wished to reduce France to barbarism. For France has been the country of all countries which has set her face against the chaos which is the devil's natural kingdom. It is against France, our Christian and chivalrous France, with its love and its laughter and its ability to remedy the many ills from which it suffers still, that our enemy has incited those more primitive peoples whose culture is small and whose hearts are savage. Nor is the harm our enemy does merely a material harm. He sets out to corrupt our countrymen's souls, till they join forces with the enemies of France. Against this twofold attack we need to defend ourselves . . . we need to pray.'

Gildas, sitting on the right, faced the crowded nave. Over men's shoulders and between women's head-dresses, from time to time he caught glimpses of Anna's calm and attentive face. As the preacher spoke of those who would come back changed of soul or no more than the shell of the men they once had been, Gildas had watched her with increased intensity. It seemed that for her the words held no foreboding. He was exultant : ' She loves me—she does love me. She trusts me in everything. She's only afraid that I'll be killed. She hasn't any other doubts.'

Continuing, the priest spoke of the men of that parish who had fallen for France and of the good example set by the women who had taken their places and worked the farms in their stead. He bade the children help their mothers ; he exhorted all to have a generous spirit : let each (he said) be prepared for every kind of sacrifice ; let each be prompt to obey God's call—which is the call to compassion ; let each give that service which in times of testing in the past has proved the salvation of France ! His last words were these :

' Soon this great ruin around us must be made good. Soon France will need priests in great numbers. Already many have been killed. To find new recruits for the priesthood will not be easy. Even before the war this was not easy. For this the Great Sower is not to blame. It is man's fallow soul that is at fault. You have all noticed how lavish God is with seed. To increase and multiply is the first law of nature, and this multiplication goes on almost to infinity. Human folly and natural accidents are always lessening the abundance given of God.

' So it is with the priestly vocation. God plants it in many souls. The indifferent, the spiritually deaf, the obstinately wicked—all kill it in their turn. Often it is killed by the neglect of parents who in their blindness have discouraged it. A day shall come when the great host of saints-who-might-have-been shall rise and denounce the parents who, blind or perverted, were guilty of this murder ! Young people and little children who, sitting here by the side of parents innocent of such offences, are listening to me now : if you have heard God's call, no matter when, no matter where, let not your ears be deaf to it ! Though it be true that the call came to you long ago, your response to it may be even now not too late. There may be obstacles : you are not asked to remove them by your own unaided strength. In their removal you will have the help of our Great Master, who has time without end at his disposal and means of whose nature and number we can have no idea. If, however, you have not yet a sense of vocation and therefore no opportunity of response to it, carefully examine yourselves ! The sacerdotal vocation is hard to follow : because it is hard it is a lovely thing. Nor is that all. It is lovely because it concerns the saving of souls ; it is lovely because it is upon this call to those who love God truly and unselfishly that the salvation of France herself depends ! '

During the sermon Anna, in her place second from the end of the Maguern pew, had sat very stiff and straight. From time to time she arranged her cloak lest she should crease her dress. Gildas no longer looked her way. Some inward emotion had left his eyes downcast and stern and his face disturbed. He tried to recall the voice which he had heard when he was ten years old : ' You shall be my priest,' it had declared to him with a wordlessness more eloquent than any words. He had been in the hayloft, he remembered. Pitchfork in hand, he had stood stock still, afraid lest the great happiness which had suddenly possessed him should as suddenly depart. . . .

He had told his father nothing of this call that had

come to him. To his mother, however, as she bade him good night, he had confided a few faltering words. Yet when he was next at confession he had been too timid to confide in his priest. In fact it had been years before his courage was equal to the confession, while more years had passed since he had made it. Had he been wrong ? Could he, a mere farm boy, his father's drover and labourer, have left his work, his home, and his own country in order to study at the seminary at Ploërmel or at S. Anne's ? Who could have found his fees ? His family was not well-to-do. Surely the Voice had overlooked this when it had declared to a Breton farm boy : ' You shall be my priest ! '

This too he remembered : with that moment's moving joy he had known at the same time the utter conviction that, though in the future he might be tempted to deny this, he had been the victim of no illusion. He had not forgotten how he had said to himself, ' I have never been saner in my life, nor happier, nor more sure of my soul than I was a moment ago when I heard the Voice and its message for me.'

The priest had left the pulpit. Accompanied by the harmonium, the congregation sang the creed. Gildas did not join in the singing. Leaning slightly forward, he stood very still. Busy with thoughts of the past, questioning his conscience of the present, he grew increasingly troubled. His thoughts came crowding : ' I didn't scoff at the Voice ; I didn't refuse to listen, but it seemed to be asking the impossible of me. It was some time before I mentioned it at confession ; for I was young and shy. Perhaps it was wrong to be shy. At first only mother knew, and she knows no more of things outside her day's work than I do. I hoped the

Voice would speak a second time. And so I waited. But though I never forgot it, I never heard it again. Now I am a grown man, old enough to think of a wife, and I know someone who loves me. . . .'

Straightening himself, he looked towards Anna's pew. Between the head-dresses of two neighbours he saw her own, whose white diadem seemed to him a shining star in a dark sky. He saw too her face uplifted and tranquil as she sang the *Credo*.

'And I—I love her very much : I'm sure we shall be happy together. Yet whenever I think of her, I remember the Voice, and am afraid. Is it right for me to make a match of it with Anna ? Or is it wrong ? It's true that I'm too old to start studying now and in any case I've got to go to the war. . . . Just now it'll be best for me to say nothing. She'll be grieved, but better she than God. It's only another week before I go. If I come back safely, I'll have seen more of life than ever I shall on a farm in a small place like this. Perhaps by that time the Voice won't be forever worrying me. Things will be different and I shall be free. Father'll say : "It's time you settled down, my boy ! " and I'll answer : "You've no need to look far for my wife. The girl I want is Anna and she's here already." I'll say to Anna : "Go and buy yourself the finest head-dress you can see. Go and buy the white silk kerchief. And if you've got the apron laid away in your chest " (I'm very sure she will have), "fetch it out for our wedding. I don't care if the girls where we will live say it's not in the fashion ! " '

'Poor Anna ! I can guess what her surprise is. I am sure she has bought the most expensive apron in Muzillac to please me, and in a minute——'

The tinkling of a bell roused Gildas from his reverie. The priest was elevating the Host. Confused, the young man bent his head in reverence. Until Mass was over, he did not again glance across the aisle to see in her place near the edge of the nave the girl whose fair beauty was the fairer and more beautiful because of the purity of her face in prayer.

The service finished. By the transept door and by the door at the middle of the nave, the congregation filed out to meet among the tombstones which looked towards the distant sea. From the churchyard walls gardens sloped down to houses in the lower part of the town. Beyond these were green fields dotted with broom bushes, while in the distance a forest of magnificent trees stood clear against the horizon. Near Billiers the serrated rocks stood out through the gap, and a shining blur marked the sea. With this before them the crowd scattered. Here and there among the stone and wooden crosses reverent figures knelt to show their respect for some dead relative. Most of the congregation, including Anna, her aunt, and Armandine, skirted the side of the church and reached the inn by way of the small square. The three women halted on the right of the churchyard gate.

Anna unfastened the black cloak, which Armandine took from her and rolled up. All could now see the new apron, magnificent with its red velvet and embroidered silk flowers, that Anna had bought in secret for her lover's sake. The streaming sunshine fell full upon her queenly head-dress, upon her fair hair plaited in two coils, upon her eyes with their high light of pride, and upon her chin whose smallness hinted at gentle birth. It glittered too upon the small gold cross at her neck and upon the cherry-coloured velvet which lay rich against her long skirt of black wool. Anna's clothes were the talk of the day. A dozen or more Muzillac women and as many Muzillac girls, forgetting their haste to reach home, retraced their steps to gaze at them, while others behind quickened their pace.

Armandine went first carrying the cloak; Anna and her aunt walked behind, nodding and smiling; for there was no one with whom they were not acquainted. There were whisperings on all sides; heads were craned in their direction: 'Isn't it pretty! Look, Rosalie!'—'Do look, Eugénie! It's real velvet.'—'And doesn't she carry it well!'

Gildas was by no means the last to see this magnificence. Before Anna's coming he had waited with two younger companions in the square to the left of the churchyard gate. She drew near, walking by her aunt's side and suiting her steps to the older woman's. His mother, it was plain, did not know whether to laugh or to be annoyed by the crowd. To Gildas Anna seemed lovelier by far than the clothes she wore. As for her, she had eyes for none but him. The delight in her smile said more plainly than words: 'Admit that you're pleased with my surprise! I've planned it only for you. My earnings for a year have gone for this. These Muzillac folk approve of me—that's obvious. But— do you?'

Yet even as she smiled her delight, she noticed that he had been content for his companions to push in front of him, so that he himself was half hidden behind them. She noticed too that, despite his unconcealed admiration, he did not look happy, but seemed to be struggling with some inward perplexity.

' Aren't you coming with us ? ' she said as she passed.

She made no attempt to lower her voice, and there were many who heard the words above the pealing of the bells. Anna was convinced that a moment more would see him leave his companions and join her. Then they would walk along together, and would receive the compliments and greetings of their friends. They would hear folk whisper : ' What a handsome couple ! '—' They must be sweethearts.'—' She's a smart girl.'

His answer came quickly :

' I can't. I've got to get Bounce. I'll see you down the hill.'

He turned as he spoke. Almost touching her as he passed, he disappeared by the narrow sloping path which followed the graveyard wall. Anna's face grew white. Without further attempt to answer the remarks made to her out of either curiosity or jealousy or affection, Anna crossed the square and through narrow streets reached the market-place. Eager to be with Gildas again, she made for the inn. Breathless, her aunt said :

' Don't be in such a hurry, my dear ! '

' Well, we've got to get home.'

' There's plenty of time. It's not late yet.'

With a strange inward look upon her face as of one groping and bewildered, Anna answered :

' Perhaps it's too late, aunt ; too late for me.'

This was more than the older woman could understand. Nevertheless she plodded wearily on. In her, self-sacrifice had become second nature. Characteristically she hurried, though she did not understand the need for hurry.

Anna's strained white face, contrasting oddly with

her holiday clothes, caught the attention of housewives as, returning from Mass, they stood about to open their doors. At this window and that a curtain was drawn aside. Women and girls walking leisurely greeted the Maguerns as Anna overtook them, only to feel hurt when their greetings were disregarded. It was the general opinion that such haste could be explained only by a fire or a death at Penmur farm.

In the big market-square more girls were waiting, including those who had crowded round Anna on her way to church. Two parties of them stood outside the 'Rose.' Hand in hand they marched forward, determined that this time neither the girl nor her fine clothes should escape them. Surrounding her, they forced her to walk more slowly; while she had to smile a little as she said : ' Don't hinder us ; we're in a great hurry ! '

Disregarding this appeal, they pressed about her, fingering the cloth, admiring its sheen in the sun, measuring how much material had been used, and even picking up the hem to judge for themselves of the light weight and the delicate texture of the pleated cherry-coloured velvet.

' You bought it at Delien's, didn't you, Anna ? '

' How much did you give for it ? I've never seen better velvet ! '

' The church banner itself hasn't a finer sheen ! '

' Why are you wearing it to-day for the first time ? '

' It's because of Gildas Maguern, I'll bet. Look, Anna ! Here he comes ! '

' Look out there ! Stand clear of Bounce all of you ! '

Gildas came round the corner of the square, driving the Penmur waggonette. He had used the whip to the

mare, and with his damaged wrist he had considerable
difficulty in controlling her.

' Look out,' he called again, as he stood in his seat.
Shrieking, the women scattered. Using his sound arm,
with a violent effort he drew up at the spot where the
group of girls had been talking a moment before. The
wheel of the waggonette grazed Anna Maguern, who
alone (to the secret admiration of Gildas) had stood her
ground. Marie Maguern's pride in her son's skill turned
to fear as she hurriedly drove before her Armandine and
three other small girls all dressed in their holiday clothes.

' Jump in, mother ! '

She saw that his face was as resolute as his father's
was at certain times. Accustomed to obey, she gave
Armandine her hand to help the child reach the high
step of the waggonette, and clambered in behind her.
Anna, bent on sitting beside Gildas again, had mounted
already from the other side. To chorused farewells and
still further compliments shouted by the girls of Muzillac,
the mare set off at a fast trot.

At the bridge over the stream which flows from
Penmur Pool Gildas allowed Bounce to slacken to a
slow jog trot.

Anna pressed close to his side. Bending so that she
might not be overheard, she asked :

' What's the matter with you ? '

' Nothing ! ' He said the one word tonelessly.

' You snubbed me, Gildas. Did you mean it ? '

' No ! '

With three fingers, as if she were taking the Father,
the Son and the Holy Ghost to witness, she touched
the cherry-coloured velvet, and said :

' Look ! I bought it for you. I wanted to look nice

before you went away. I wanted you to be proud
of Anna.'

' You're a pretty girl, Anna—that's certain ! '

He did not look at her as he spoke the words. His
face was turned away, his eyes fixed on far horizons.
His expression was as bleak as the wind which the
sunshine of Christmas Day had not power enough
to warm.

Anna, turning her head a little, said over her shoulder :

' I'm cold, Armandine.'

Her young cousin passed the cloak, which she had
carried over her arm since they had come out of church.
Anna drew it round her, taking care to leave it unfastened. Between the black folds, now that there was
none to see it, the apron glowed red and beautiful. The
mare went jog-jogging on.

Not wishing to be overheard, Anna bent forward
and said :

' We've got to talk. Time's precious, and there's not
much left. You'll hurt me if you go away like this, and
afterwards I shall feel worse about it. It's not that I'm
too poor for you—you told me so on the moor. And it's
not because I'm older than you—you said so yourself.
So what is it, Gildas—that's what I want to know. If
you were a quarter as fond of me as I am of you, you'd
be looking at me and not at Bounce. Other people seem
to think that I'm not such a fright ! '

Emotion had tightened the muscles of his face and
neck. Sorrow made his expression wooden. Again she
broke in upon his silence.

' For the dear Lord's sake, answer me ! '

He said no word.

' For S. Anne of Auray's sake, answer ! '

' Anna, you heard what the preacher said in church ?
About parents, I mean.'

' Why, yes ! He said that if their sons wanted to be
priests, they should let them. But you don't want to—
so what's that to do with it ? '

He lashed at Bounce with the whip. As the mare
broke into a gallop, he murmured :

' Perhaps I do.'

After a second's pause he went on :

' Anna, I'm afraid ; I'm afraid ! '

' But you're much too old, Gildas. You should have
begun as a boy. Then you would have learnt Latin.
Why you can't even say *Dominus vobiscum* properly.
But you aren't a boy—you're a grown man going to the
war. You're off your head, Gildas ! So that was why
you didn't answer ? '

' Yes ! '

' Or look at me ? '

' Yes ! '

' So you're not fond of another girl, after all ? '

' No, of course not ! '

' I'm glad—you don't know how glad I am ! You
love me and I love you. That's all that matters. That's
all we need bother about. Anything else is just waste
of time. I'm here if you want something to think about.
Oh, I feel so happy ! Don't look in front of you ! Look
at me ! '

In her heart's new-found gaiety she laughed with the
gladness of youth. In her joy she had raised her voice :
Armandine, overhearing her warm words, began to
laugh and her mother to grumble softly between jolts
of the waggonette.

' It seems to me those two don't care what time we get

home ! Here I say, Gildas ! Can't you whip Bounce up
a bit ? I've got buckwheat cakes to make for your
Christmas dinner.'

'That's good ! ' Armandine said.

'Father'll be grumbling at us, you know, Gildas ! '

Bounce began to gallop like a young colt. At the
same fast pace she turned off the Vannes road. The
waggonette came near to overturning, and there were
shrieks and laughter. The rest of the way was dear and
familiar. Here were the first Penmur fields with the
moor immediately beyond, while from behind a leafless
coppice the roof of the house appeared.

'Oh, I am happy ; I am happy ! ' Anna repeated in a
whisper. 'Turn round to me.'

But her laughter quickly lost its gaiety. For though
Gildas had looked at her, after a moment he had looked
away. She sought his eyes, but he continued to look
straight before him. She drew farther from him—yet
not too far !—and as if she were cold, fastened the
first clasp of her black woollen cloak. From her waist
the glowing velvet was hidden ; above, it shone in the
sun. If she hoped that by her movement she would
attract his attention, her hope went unrealised. Gildas
remained lost in his dreaming, to whose secret she had no
key. Suddenly she felt forlorn—forlorn and hopeless
like an old woman who loves a young man. Bounce, her
stable in sight above the low hedges dividing the road
from the moor, dropped into walking pace.

'Here we are, Armandine—back again ! ' Gildas said.

The small girl laughed at him ; Anna remained sad
and silent. When she saw, as they passed, the soft earth
and the grass where they had talked the evening before,
she felt two great tears well in her eyes. One trickled

down upon her left shoulder, and fell upon the dress. Furtively she wiped it away, at the same time fastening the other clasps of the cloak. She was now dressed as she had been when they set out, and Jean-Guillaume saw no more of the cherry-coloured velvet than he had seen earlier in the day. Standing in the yard with his hat far back on his head, he waved to them as they came in sight, smiling and nodding with pleasure at their return.

That Christmas Day of 1915 was far from joyful for those at Penmur farm. Even the buckwheat cakes did little to lessen the gloom which had fallen upon Anna, Gildas and his mother. Only a word here and there of the murmured talk of the young people on the homeward journey had been heard by the older woman, inclined to deafness as she was. Yet she had noticed the small response made by Gildas to Anna's questions. That night as the boys went to their room, his mother said to him :

' You're sad at leaving us and Anna—that's plain, my son. You're not yourself. You've scarcely looked at her all day. I suppose you're worried because you think she won't be here when you come back. But don't worry ! It's true father's anxious and not making much, and he may say that we must do without a servant. But I'll manage that—leave it to me ! Take my word for it—she shan't go before you're back ! '

In half an hour there was darkness outside. Inside, a darkness of spirit had settled upon the Penmur household. Anna, who had served dinner, washed the dishes and put back the long forms and chairs, went to give Denise her customary good night kiss. Her head was drooping and her eyes closed with weariness, as in silence she put up her mouth. Denise kissed her tenderly, and said :

'Gildas thought you were lovely, darling—and you are !'

'Do you really think he did ?' Anna answered.

Denise laughed with the quiet good-humour with which women laugh when they exchange such confidences as this.

'He told me he did !'

'When ?'

'Just now. And what's more, he said he didn't want to look at you too often, as it might make him lose heart. He meant about going, poor chap. . . .'

Anna again kissed her cousin. This time she did not droop.

CHAPTER V

PARTING

BRIGHT cold days with frost at night ended the year. By the afternoon most of the magic of those frosty nights had melted in the sun, save for the thin flakes of ice in the puddles, and the glittering border of frost on the dead leaves and the clods.

The Penmur men left the farm at dawn and were not seen again at the house until the gathering mists, grown massed and thick, rolled down upon the fields, and a premature dusk ended the day. Pigeons were in every field, grass and arable alike. Disturbed by Jean-Guillaume and his two sons as they opened or closed a gate, they rose in flocks. Turning and circling higher and higher in the wind they eventually disappeared, making for the safety of remoter and more misty fields.

The wheeling birds set each of the three busy with his own thoughts. 'It's the beginning of a hard winter,' the father reflected.—' In a day or two's time I shall be off in the direction they've come from,' Gildas told himself. The younger boy had the instincts of a poacher : it was with a poacher's craft that he watched the birds' flight, and made his calculations as to the bush or hedge which would best have served his purpose.

They went their unhurried way to the work which

they had planned to do. On the evening before Jean-Guillaume had said suddenly : ' Last year we chopped our neighbours' wood for them. The war's still on— we'll do it again this. Life's hard enough on the women left behind, without them going short of fuel.'

They did this work for the women and children on the slope of a small hill out of sight of the farm and at some distance from Penmur Pool. The two boys, climbing the trees, lopped the branches with their pruning-knives. Their father trimmed the fallen wood and tied it into bundles. Leaving this, he tidied the hedges and with his spade cleaned the choked ditches of slush and of the dead leaves which for years had accumulated there.

Usually they ate where they worked, sitting on the ground with their backs to the wind. On days of heavy rain, however, or out of courtesy, they went into the farm for whose absent owner they had been working. If possible, Jean-Guillaume avoided this ; for these soldiers' wives, left alone with their children, depressed him. As they gave him his meal, their talk of the war, little as they knew of it, left him saddened. It was the talk less of wives who were than of widows who were to be. Invariably their talk turned his thoughts to Pol already in the trenches and to Gildas who would soon be gone. Unlike their father, Gildas and Ange listened eagerly to the women's tales of their men, poignant as some of these were. For the boys had not yet looked upon death, and for them such tales had all the interest of fiction.

After a day spent in this work their tramp home was long and tedious, because of Jean-Guillaume's great weariness. Trying to laugh, the old man would say : ' I can't think how I'll manage when you're gone, Gildas.

You do half the work, my son.' Or again, as they came
to a stile, he would remark : ' It's a good thing you're
here to help your old father, Gildas ! '—' I shall be here,
shan't I ? ' Ange would protest. Banter would pass
between the brothers, making the way less weary, as
their laughter echoed over the quiet fields. Thick mists
continued : each night they stumbled over clods or
went astray from the path. Here and there in the
meadows' grassy hollows they would startle a sleeping cow
into a wild lowing gallop ; for in some farms the women
had no boy old enough to drive the cattle home to their
byre, and so were obliged to leave the beasts in the
open, winter though it was. What they would have
done without the fodder of the fields they dared not
think.

Before they reached the farm it would be pitch-black.
Across the yard a stream of light would pour from the
open door of the living-room : in this light dust and
wisps of straw floated and disappeared. Every few
minutes the immense shadow of a woman peering out of
the door would fall across this luminous tunnel.

' Aren't they coming yet, Anna ? '

' No, Aunt Marie.'

' You can't hear anything ? '

' Only a dog S. Gourlais way, and the wind in the
trees.'

' Come along in, then.'

The men would come in shortly afterwards, tired and
it might be drenched with rain. Their words to the
women were terse and abrupt. They were hungry ;
they were cold. As Anna brought their meal she tried
to appear serene and happy. She made cheerful remarks
or humorous sallies, as she told the men of the day's

gossip. No one paid heed to what she said, unless it were the children ; for the grown-ups were preoccupied with what the future might bring. When Anna poured a glass of cider for Gildas, or when she passed him a plate, she made no haste to withdraw her roughened but delicate hand. She remembered how often he had looked at it in the past, and had lifted his eyes to smile into her face. Her face had not changed, yet now he did not look up. She herself had not changed, yet now all her hold upon him, it seemed, was gone.

Gildas' last evening arrived. At prayers after supper Anna knelt next to him, gently pushing Armandine aside to make room for herself. She and Gildas were so close that their shoulders touched. When they made the sign of the cross together, they might well have been a married couple, who in church are privileged to kneel very near together and even to lean each against the other, as if to show how sweet marriage seems to them. He made no attempt to draw himself away from her. She heard the rich inflections of her beloved's voice, that ranged effortlessly from the low pitch of his father's bass to his own more youthful tenor.

Prayers said, Jean-Guillaume began an *Ave Maria* ' for our son Gildas who goes to the war.' Anna felt Gildas take her hand and clasp it tight. After the Amen she heard him say in a whisper meant for her alone : ' It's hard to leave you, dear ! '

How her heart rejoiced ! Hastily she got to her feet, and in the hope of talking with Gildas would have gone with him either to the quiet of the farmyard or at least to the chimney corner with its promise of privacy. For her great need was to unburden her heart of the love which had so long oppressed it. But already Ange,

Alexis, and Armandine were crowding about their brother who was to go early on the following morning; while from beyond the small group which they made, their mother came forward and drew her son to her, saying :

' Poor boy, you are very tired ! But still, come into our room for a moment and say good-bye.'

He followed her. Jean-Guillaume was for the moment busy in the stable. Under the dormer window through which a stream of wind from the farmyard flowed icily, they took their seats upon a rickety and worm-eaten chest in which Marie Maguern kept her cast-off head-dresses, a silver chain, a black velvet kerchief and a small wooden horse belonging to a boy whom she had lost years before. In front of them in a kind of cubby-hole no bigger than a ship's cabin stood the old people's bed.

Beneath the diminutive copper lamp, with face drawn close to his, the mother sat looking at her son. From his candid eyes he looked back at her.

' Gildas, morning and evening and often in between I shall pray God to keep you safe—you know that ! In your new life there'll be many temptations ! '

' Yes, mother, I suppose so.'

' There'll be many you can't trust, especially women.'

She looked at the face which she loved. Beneath his fair moustache she noticed the suspicion of a smile.

' Why do you smile when I say " especially women," Gildas ? '

' Because I know that already.'

Her face became anxious.

' Yes, even here in the country, no doubt, a boy like you must be careful. But from what they say, in cities and towns it's far worse, particularly for a Christian.

Go where you have to ! There's no need to be a boor, but you can keep away from women. You never know what the young ones are up to. They're always setting traps.'

' Always, mother ? '

Now Gildas' smile became a laugh, and his mother knew that his thoughts were of the girl he loved. She looked at him knowingly. Wagging her head and screwing up her eyes, she said :

' Perhaps you mean somebody round here ? '

She alluded to Anna, remembering significant words and looks that had passed between them during the previous three years. At the same moment the memory came to her of a remark made by him in that same room during his choir-boy days : ' It's a fine thing to be a priest, mother ! ' he had said.—' Perhaps you mean somebody round here ? ' Despite its wording, the question had been direct. She wondered what answer he would make.

' As I'm going, mother, perhaps—— '

She was not to be thwarted, however, and said :

' You're going, I know ; but you'll come back, and then—well, we all know what a dear girl Anna is ! '

He tried to speak, but failed. Big tears glittered on his eye-lashes.

' We'll look after her, Gildas—you can be sure of that,' she continued.

She kissed him and clasped him to her, and in a broken voice told him to remember the prayers and the principles which he had been taught at Penmur, not to forget his duty and to obey his superior officers.

Getting up from the chest, in low tones in which filial respect and pride were mingled he gave his mother the promise she asked. She could trust a Maguern, he said, to do his duty.

As he left his mother and opened the door to the living-room, Jean-Guillaume, coming in from the yard, called : ' Gildas, where's Gildas ? '

In the first box-bed Denise was already asleep ; Anna sat at the foot of hers, finishing a knitted waistcoat that she was making for Gildas. The dim lamp left much of the large room in shadow, while the fire was dead grey ash. As Gildas came forward to meet his father, Anna rose, throwing her knitting upon the waxed chest.

' I've given the mare her feed,' she heard her uncle say. ' Sleep well, my boy, on your last night at home ! Don't worry ! I'll call you in the morning. I'm coming with you. Ange wanted to, but I said no. Now that you're going there's more than enough for him to do here ! '

Gildas went straight to Anna. As earlier at prayers, he took her hand, clasping it tight. From his greater height he leaned towards her, that the others in their beds might not overhear. He murmured :

' Don't get up to-morrow, dear, to see me off ! I shall go out by the stable way. I know that they'll think of me, when I'm out there ; but it's you I ask to pray for me. Pray every day—for I have a feeling that if you miss a day I shall be killed.'

' Then you'll be safe, Gildas ! '

' Good-bye, Anna ! '

' Good-bye, Gildas ! '

Her eyes never left him as he walked to the far end of the room, and disappeared into the boys' bedroom. ' But it's you I ask to pray for me. . . .' Upon her pretty face the memory of his murmured words set a soft light of happiness. It gave her satisfaction that she had contrived not to cry. Soon she would be in her bed, and then none would see her tears.

On a chair Gildas found his candle. Quickly undressing, by its light he saw that his two brothers were asleep. On a second chair his small case stood open, full to overflowing with his clothes and parcels of food. The inside straps scarcely met round its bulging contents. Upon a woollen waistcoat a picture had been stitched : he recognised S. Anne, Brittany's patron saint, and told himself that in the coming July her feast day on the twenty-sixth of the month would find Gildas Maguern far away. . . .

It was still dark when Jean-Guillaume, as he had promised, came to wake his son. Only his wife, whom grief had kept from sleep, heard him open the stable door leading into the boy's room. The trap was made ready and its lantern lit. Jean-Guillaume had taken the precaution of tying the mare to the chicken-house door so that she would not disturb the household by her prancing and pawing on the gravel.

Father and son took their seats. Gildas had one foot on the step when his mother came out in cloak and hood to give him a last embrace. ' Good-bye, my dear boy ! ' she said. Then looking at the sky to see the wild scurrying of the clouds over the stars, she added : ' Turn up your coat-collar, son ! There'll be a lot of wind on the Vannes road.' As Jean-Guillaume picked up the reins, Gildas said with a laugh : ' I shan't have anybody to tell me that over there.' They were his farewell words. She smiled at him that this parting might be a little easier for them both. She watched the trap till it was out of sight.

As Gildas had wished, Anna had kept indoors. Her heart's mysterious prompting had wakened her at the moment of his going. With her left hand she lifted her bed curtains. Through the window she saw a light— a light like a star—grow small and then smaller until the distance swallowed it.

CHAPTER VI

NEWS

IN most cases men from Brittany were sent to either the Tenth or the Eleventh Army Corps. Some, however, were posted to the Ninth, which had suffered severe losses since August 1914. Accordingly, acting on the call-up notice which he had received from Vannes recruiting station on January 5, Gildas Maguern presented himself at Angers. His country hat, cardboard attaché case and uncertain manner plainly marked him as a recruit. Hesitatingly he asked the station-master where the barracks lay, to receive only a curt : ' Sorry, my man ! I'm busy ! ' He then enquired again of the girl clerk at the platform book-stall who merely said : ' You'll have to wait till I've finished here.' The attention of the military policeman on duty was caught by these questions. He directed Gildas to take a Paris tram passing the station.

On the long ride to the immense new barracks of the 135th Regiment, which stood on the hill at the far end of the town, Gildas noticed that civilians were in the habit of giving up their seats to men in uniform. Within a quarter of an hour of leaving the tram he was posted to his company, and shortly afterwards was given full kit. That night he slept in a half-empty barrack-room. His

case was above him on the high shelf that ran the full
length of the whitewashed wall.

Next morning, with three other recruits, he was given
his first drills by a corporal whose favourite form of
address for Gildas was either ' blooming bumpkin ' or
' blasted Breton ' (the corporal's father was a sewer-
man). From Parade to Retreat he browbeat the young
soldier and put him through each drill a score of times.
At the final ' Dismiss ' Gildas invited the corporal to a
neighbouring café. Here he put things on a more
friendly footing by sharing with him a bottle of
' Bordeaux ' (or so the label described it) and half a
dozen cigars.

For Gildas the first weeks in barracks were weeks of
no small hardship. Essentially of respectable parentage
and of strict Christian upbringing, suddenly this country
boy found himself deprived of all his customary supports.
He was wistful for Brittany and sore at heart for the
Breton sea and the Breton men who sailed upon it. He
felt alone and forsaken. Hungry for friendship, he had
no friend nor knew where he might find one. He had the
Breton suspiciousness, and when two or three of his
comrades, unknown to him even by name, asked him
to go with them into the town, he would not join
them.

Even if they were going merely for a stroll, he knew
that meant drinks, and he could not afford to buy drinks.
For his money was almost gone, and on no account
would he ask for more from home. Already his father
was crippling himself in order to keep two husbandless
women and several children. Again he found small
pleasure in the occasional visits which he made alone to
cafés : the cider, he found, was poor watery stuff

compared with the good home-brew made from the Muzillac apples. On the other hand the theatre—by the theatre he meant the cinema and those smoking concerts which soldiers were free to attend—appealed to a certain adventurous streak in him. Nevertheless from the ' theatre ' he stayed away, since both his mother at home and the rector at church had spoken of the dangerous temptations which lurked there.

Then there were women—the kind of women he had no wish to know. About these women men who were granted night-passes made obscene remarks and bawdy jokes. The two strong pillars of his early training had been piety and purity. Certain details left him so revolted that it seemed to him that a soul within his soul sat on a high place pronouncing judgement upon this new life of his. He remembered the clean sweetness of his old life, none of whose memories brought him any sense of remorse, and compared it with things that he either saw or guessed at around him, and with those other things of which he read or could not fail to hear.

Vivid pictures of Penmur that came to him when he was alone gave him strength. In fancy he was back with his father and mother and sisters ; he was once more with his boyhood friends ; he walked and talked again with Anna in her maiden's simplicity and woman's wisdom. In his heart he gave her thanks for what she had given to him, and to his secret soul acknowledged, as he had never before acknowledged, that Anna was the kind of woman a man was wise to love, since in her was no evil nor suspicion of evil. She had been so much in his thought that on one occasion he had answered the ' Where do you come from, chum ? ' with ' From Anna's country.' ' You mean Brittany ! ' the other

had said, thinking that he referred to its patron saint.
' That's it,' he had answered confusedly.

At intervals he wrote brief letters to Penmur. His mind
was very active, but none but God knew its workings.
He was not always concerned with the past. For in
those days, with the imaginative in particular, it was
the future rather than the past which occupied men's
thoughts, the immediate future, which meant the
war.

Newspapers, forbidden in barracks, were read when
men went into the town. There were innumerable
rumours : hospital orderlies who picked them up from
the wounded were one rich source of these. Again, Red
Cross nurses would chat to an officer in the course of
their duties, or more occasionally with some private
whom they chanced to know. Whether this gossip was
of a general or news of some subaltern back from the
front, whether of hospital trivialities or of details of the
latest battle, it was eagerly circulated. The merest
trifles of these nurses' conversation were commented on
at length.

In the evening some of the men would read the com-
muniqués posted outside the police-station in their glass
case and under wire grating. In such ways these men,
who had left field and factory, workshop and office desk
that in arms they might save France from final defeat by
the invader, had glimpses of the perils of war which they
were soon to share.

Sick for the home which was denied him, Gildas was
eager to be sent to the front. Because he differed from
his fellows he was considered unsociable. Because he
spoke little and that little in a not uncultured voice, his
comrades were jealous and critical of him. They knew

that like themselves he had had no more than an elementary education. Yet they could not ignore the delicacy of his features or his sensitive spirit, or that self-restraint which so often is the mark of good-breeding. Jealousy of this farmer's boy from rural Muzillac found its frequent expression in such remarks as ' That chap's no better than us, yet he gives himself an officer's airs and graces.' In this they were wrong : he did not give himself those airs—he had them. Such superiority, though it be suspected rather than evident, is an offence in the eyes of the mean-spirited. Towards the end of May, when Gildas had completed five months' training, a barrack-room incident proved that some of his companions were of this order.

On the staff was an officer who might well have been Gildas' elder brother. He had the same height, the same delicate build, the same outward timidity hiding the same inherent strength and courage. The effects of a bullet-wound in the left leg received in Belgium in the 1914 fighting had given him a limp. This officer had asked to be sent back to the trenches, but had been kept at the base. Though engaged in clerical work he did his share in maintaining discipline, since at that time the barracks were badly understaffed. As he limped along painfully with the aid of his walking-stick he was often to be seen about his duties in the square or on the staircases of the barracks.

At about five o'clock on a particular evening Gildas' section were in the barrack-room brushing their clothes before going into the town. Gildas was stooping to change his muddy army boots when a recruit, a sunburned and garrulous fellow who had come in from Béziers only a week before, struck him and sent him sprawling. He had chosen the wrong man. Gildas got to his feet, saying:

' Do you want a tanning, you little rat ? '

The other retreated between the two rows of beds as Gildas advanced upon him. The rest of the section made a ring about the pair, leaving them sufficient space to fight it out. The Southerner, however, had no fight in him. He tried to arouse feeling against Gildas by shouting:

' I only gave him a little push. He won't be so lucky next time. You chaps had better keep your eye on him ! He tells everyone he's fed up with the barracks. He thinks he'll get in the officers' good books that way. We'll be sent to the trenches before we're due to go.'

' You're a liar, Marius ! '

' You stay there, Gildas ! Stop him, boys ! He wants to do me in ! '

Marius had by this time backed almost to the wall. The men laughed and jeered. Gildas lifted a boot and let fly at him. Marius shrieked and ducked as it came hurtling at him, narrowly missing his head. It crashed against the wall, falling on one of the beds amid a cloud of whitewash. There were cheers from the men who looked on and who now intervened to prevent further violence. During a scuffle in which laughter played the biggest part, the door was opened and the lieutenant entered.

' Attention ! ' the corporal bawled, though he himself was in the thick of the scrimmage.

The men stood to attention at the foot of the beds, while the officer demanded an explanation. Though scarcely more than a boy, he showed a grave impassivity that no judge could have bettered. As the corporal explained how the fracas had begun, he looked now at Marius, whose face was as red as one of his own red southern wines, and now at Gildas, whose angry pallor persisted as he continued to glare, while his fingers twitched to set about the other.

'You, corporal, and you, Gildas Maguern, stay where you are! The rest of you, dismiss!'

They tramped heavily down the stairs, leaving the three men in the barrack-room. The lieutenant came up to Gildas: 'Come and look at the mess you've made!'

Leading him to the wall between Marius's bed and his neighbour's, he pointed out the muddy imprint of the boot on the white surface. Using his finger-tip, he counted the indentations one by one:

'Twenty-seven! you can see the bare stone in twenty-seven different places. You might have killed the man! Now listen to me! You're keen—we know that. The draft is off very shortly, and then you'll be able to show what you're made of. You'll be able to distinguish yourself out there, but it won't be against your comrades. Now you're to get some whitewash and a brush, and to work away till there's no trace of that mess. I'll be back in an hour to inspect, and you'll get as many days C.B. as there are dents in the wall.'

At the end of the hour above Marius's bed the wall was whiter and smoother than it had been when the building was new.

The incident made a lasting impression on the minds both of Gildas and of the men of his section. Gildas was secretly ashamed at the thought of the anger which had surprised and mastered him. At Penmur, life had been

patriarchal : in the army Gildas knew for the first time
what it was to be an equal among equals. He needed,
he discovered, to be on his guard against the violence of
an excitable nature and to strive for a far greater measure
of self-mastery. On the following day, outwardly calm,
he forced himself to apologise to the Béziers man. The
Southerner, knowing himself to have been the aggressor,
was astonished that Gildas made no reference to the
fact. At heart good-humoured, he was touched by
the apology. Equally, the other men, impressed by
Gildas' ability to give rather better than he got, had
considerable respect for him, coupled with a certain
healthy fear.

Some days later, at the beginning of June, Gildas was
sent with a draft to an infantry battalion lying in
support on the Lorraine front. A letter written to his
father soon after his arrival ran :

' I am back in the fields again. We are not in the
firing line, but we soon shall be. They have sent us
trench-digging, though it is not so much trenches we dig
as ditches with a good parapet facing the enemy. I am
better than most at this digging. It is very different
soil from Penmur—you never saw such poor pebbly
stuff. At home Long Marsh is bad enough, but this is
worse. I am learning bomb-throwing, too. It is pretty
terrifying when they go off. In fact they are rather
like the sergeant-major ! Your number is up if you
get hit.

' I am not so good as some on the range. But like the
rest of the Muzillac boys I know something about shoot-
ing. Anyway, when Denise next writes to Pol, she can
tell him that yesterday I got five bulls. Good old Pol !
I wonder whether I shall see him at Verdun. It is just

possible ; for we are a reserve battalion, and they will send us where we are wanted most.

'The country here in Lorraine—at least in this part where we are—has scarcely any trees, though there are a few small woods by the fields. Ploughing goes on almost in sight of the Germans. It is enough to break your heart to see how these woods have been destroyed.

'Good-bye and give my love to everybody, especially to mother.

'Your respectful and ever-loving son,

'GILDAS.'

He had written : 'I wonder if I shall see Pol at Verdun.' This was not to be. For on June 11, when the postman handed this letter to Jean-Guillaume, as he continued his round to Savarit Farm he said :

'They've something for you at the Town Hall.'

'What's that ? '

'Some kind of form—I don't know what. You'll be going along, I suppose ? '

He went, taking the steep moor path. Jean-Guillaume had intended to cut the first oats of that year, which were putting out pale shoots, growing green already at the tip and half out of the sheath. This cutting would now need to be left until the following day.

He took his coat and started for Muzillac. At the farm the women awaited his return impatiently, each trying to conceal from the others the desperate fear in her heart. He was a long time gone.

Returning, from the doorstep he said at once :

'Poor things, it's not good news I'm bringing.'

Involuntarily his eyes had turned to Denise standing on his left. Guessing the truth, she sank to her knees, crying :

' Oh, Pol—it's Pol ! He's dead. O God, pity us both ! '

Pol was indeed dead—dead with a bullet through his heart. He had fallen at Verdun on the first of June. Jean-Guillaume's trembling fingers with difficulty unfolded the War Office form whose tragic words Denise could not bring herself to read. She had tottered to her bed, from which she muttered as she sobbed convulsively :

' Oh, my baby ! He'll have no father ! he'll have no father ! ' Anna went to her. She neither fussed nor used vain words. She put her arms round her cousin and in one simple phrase spoke all her heart :

' Poor thing ! '

At the first word of Pol's death the old mother had gone to the hearth, where she sat huddled over the fire. Mechanically she made it up as she murmured the rosary to comfort herself. Paying no heed to the rest of the household, by turns she put on coals and prayed for her son's soul.

The postman on his round quickly spread the news through the parish. At every door he would say : ' Yes, it's true, but don't spread it about. Another Muzillac man has been killed—the eldest Maguern boy.'

Before the end of the afternoon, one after another, condoling neighbours came to Penmur, all wondering how long it would be before they in their turn received such condolences. The first was Mme Voilier, a widow living by herself at Coléno Farm. Although she had a son of about forty, she might have been thought a young woman ; for her voice was soft and charming. She was tall, and always wore black clothes relieved only by her white hair and a white kerchief. Her son, who had joined the Territorials early in September, had been stationed at Verdun. She came partly to show her gratitude to Jean-Guillaume, who worked her three fields on the hillside for her, and partly to hear of Verdun which, in everybody's mouth at that time, for her had a special significance.

Was it a big town like Vannes, or smaller like Muzillac ? And if the guns continually battered it, were there any houses left where Théophile might find shelter ?

The Maguerns had been certain that their neighbours would call. When Mme Voilier came in, they were all, down to the small Armandine, sitting round the living-room, rather as if the dead man were lying in their midst, awaiting the visitors that they knew would come. In her sweet low voice that was beloved of all, Mme Voilier questioned Jean-Guillaume as to how Pol had met his death. Had it been, she wondered, in a pitched battle with fierce hand-to-hand fighting and horses galloping through clouds of smoke as you saw it in pictures ? Or had it been at some open corner for which Pol had unwisely left his cover ? ' Oh, Marguerite, I only know that he was shot through the heart,' was all that Jean-Guillaume could find to say.

In her broken voice the mother was still saying a rosary for her son. Marguerite went over to join her. She did not speak ; she did not stir. In her place by the hearth she sat opposite her husband, her heart surrendered to its grief and crying out to its God.

When she had stayed as long as was fitting, Marguerite Voilier rose to go. Jean-Guillaume, leaving his place by the fire-side, went with her to the door. There he whispered :

'If it's fine to-morrow, Marguerite, Ange and I will come and cut your lucern.'

The next to come were a brother and sister who were trying to work Lantiern Farm. The boy, unusually grave and courteous for his fifteen years, and his sister (the most beautiful girl in Muzillac, people said), a year younger than he, were a handsome pair. Their father was away at the war; their mother suffered from a creeping paralysis that prevented her from walking farther than her chicken-house or the dairy. For nearly two years past Jean-Guillaume, moved by their hard lot, had made no charge to them for the use of his labourers on their land. For despite his morose exterior the old man had a kind heart.

The two stayed no great time at Penmur, though the time seemed long to them, for to learn to bear our own sorrows, and to understand those of others, takes some time. When the door of Penmur had closed behind them they exchanged no words, but their eyes said plainly : 'We had to go, but it's a good thing it's over !'

Out of sight of the house they showed their relief in excited talk, and, like the children they were, picked bunches of wild-flowers and chased each other round the clumps of furze.

Later in the day the priest came from Muzillac. He spoke kindly to them all, and promised that he would write to the colonel of Pol's regiment, and if possible find out where the lad had been buried. 'Buried '— even now they found it hard to think of their tall and good-tempered Pol as one of that quiet host of the Verdun dead.

Last of all came the villagers. On their way home from the day's work they would leave their tools against the wall of the house, and going no further than the door would show their respect in such few comforting words as came to them. There were few but had the thought : ' Who knows ? To-morrow it may be us ! '

That night was a night of sorrow. Denise was put to bed with high fever where she groaned continually. Anna, who had lain fully dressed on her own bed, went repeatedly to give her the cool drinks for which she asked. In the third box-bed Armandine suddenly started awake, for a brief while wept, and then once more was deep in sleep.

Thus it came about that these three box-beds had become as many small chapels in which the living prayed for the dead and were themselves near to death through weariness.

Early next day Jean-Guillaume prepared for work. He drank two glasses of cider and ate a little bread. Packing some food in an old cartridge-box, he called to Alexis and Ange who were already working in the stables.

' I'm going to cut the lucern for Marguerite Voilier, as I promised. Ange, you give the beasts a little food. Not much—hay is going to be dear and the oats are being cut. They always are at the end of the season. Then you come up to the lucern field too. Now, Alexis, you take the cattle on the moor just round the house. Take Rabigo, and watch the herd and the house as well.'

He took the big scythe. Only Pol, Gildas, and he had been able to handle it, but Pol was dead ; Gildas was away in Lorraine.

About three hours later, shortly after Ange had gone over the moor with his smaller scythe to join his father, Denise in sudden pain called to Anna :

' I think I'm going to have my baby soon, Anna. Go and tell Aunt Marie—she's with the chickens down the bottom of the yard. Break it gently to her—she's too old for these shocks.'

Until midday, work at Penmur went on as usual. About noon, as Denise's pain had grown worse, Anna took Armandine to some friends who lived on the cliffs overlooking the pool. Explaining how matters were at the farm, she asked them to look after the child for the rest of that day.

Meanwhile Alexis had stabled the cattle, and at his mother's bidding started for Muzillac to fetch the mid-wife. On the doorstep Marie Maguern said to him : ' Don't stop on the way. After you've told Mme Quistrebert that we want her here at once—remember to say " at once," won't you, Alexis—run as fast as you can to your father. He's in the lucern field at Coléno. Go by the short cuts you know across the fields. Ange is there, but never mind him. He can stay. Just say to your father " Mother has some news for you—not bad news. She wants you to come home. It's the baby." '

The small boy was proud that his mother should so trust him, and trotted off down the Muzillac road. He met a boy he knew ; he saw a blackbird's nest—yet he stayed for neither. When he came to the town he went resolutely past the shop windows, and those who knew him wondered what was the matter that the young dawdler should keep up such a pace.

In the living-room of Penmur Marie Maguern hung the huge copper pot on its hook before the fire. She had first cleaned it well with a bunch of nettles. Into this she emptied two full buckets of water that she herself had drawn from the well, and had carefully skimmed with a

spoon of the broken fronds of fern and odd wisps of
wire-grass.

On her aunt's bed Anna was busy laying out linen,
napkins, and a vest which she herself had knitted.
Nor did she forget the two bows of ribbon for the cradle
—one pink if the baby were a girl, the other blue if it
were a boy. With grim humour the old woman said :
' There ought to be a black one.'

It was a girl. She was the first of the ninth generation
of Maguerns to be born in that house. She was small and
puny ; her grandmother murmured ' The little mite ! '
as she put her in the low cradle on the chest at the foot
of Denise's bed. As the first stars began to glimmer, the
family took a hasty supper in the boys' room. When the
usual prayers had been said, Jean-Guillaume asked
blessings of the family's patron saints, including S. Pol
de Léon. After a final *Ave Maria* for the new baby he
turned to his wife and said : ' What's her name to be ? '

' Denise has not said,' she answered.

Night brought peace to Penmur. Utterly weary, they
all, even Denise, were soon sound asleep. The baby
slept too, only twice before morning whimpering feebly
for a while. Even the wild Rabigo lay quiet in his
kennel. For once he did not bark at the martens ; for
once he paid no heed to those far-off noises which only he
could hear ; neither rustlings from the coppice, nor foot-
falls on the road, nor twitterings from the sky had power
to make him restless.

When the family rose next morning somewhat later
than usual, Jean-Guillaume's first thought was of what
they should name the child.

He found Denise white and unsmiling in her bed.
Going to the cradle, the old man took the baby into his

arms. He drew back the bed-curtains and held the child for her to see. She smiled at him faintly.

' Well, Denise, what's her name to be ? '

' I don't know. *He* should say that, and he . . .'

' But—if he's not here, we must choose one for him. Folks don't care for the old-fashioned names, these days. It's all Suzanne and Odette now, or else Christiane and Hélène. Let's have an old name, shall we ? '

' All right. What ? '

' Marie.'

Jean-Guillaume again held out the child to its mother. She kissed it, murmuring ' Bless you, Marie ! '

Next day the child was baptised. Although it was not a feast everyone felt happy at Penmur. Grief is fleeting ; soon Pol was half forgotten except by Denise and the old people. Even with these three the days brought work, as the nights brought weariness, and sorrow was dulled with the passing weeks. First there was the haymaking ; then the oats, the rye, the barley, and the wheat had to be gathered. At the end of the first week in August threshing began. Penmur and those other farms which Jean-Guillaume worked for their absent owners made part of the *Campbert* of S. Gourlais. Twenty-two households in all belonged to this association : to each the modern motor-driven thresher and its workers came in turn. Its coming was an event. Its shrill whistle, its long shoot and its huge elevator were talked of from one harvest to another. It arrived at each farm on a set day when, whether it was early morning or late evening, the villagers would run excitedly to see it. They gaped at the sight of the clattering monster at work, as its metal maws swallowed the sheaves and whirled the straw upwards. This year especially it seemed to fascinate Jean-Guillaume, and he missed no opportunity of watching it, usually with Ange and on three occasions with Anna.

It was the last day's threshing at Trébestan's farm. The workers, exhausted and sweating when they sat down to supper, revived as the food and wine went round. The younger men among them made ready to dance in the open. In all this there was nothing unusual or strange. Yet Anna, sitting at the end of the long supper-table, grew suddenly aware that into her uncle's manner to herself a new note of warmth and friendliness had crept. When he touched her on the shoulder, she was conscious of it; when he said, ' Coming, Anna ? ' his tones made her sure of it.

Jean-Guillaume put on his coat, which he had taken off for supper, and they left the noise and the heat of the supper-room for the starlit peace of their homeward road and the coolness of the steady breeze which blew from the south. Jean-Guillaume, familiar with the path, suited his pace to the girl's, as she followed him through stubble fields and meadows. For a while they heard the tunes on the accordion and the voices of the dancers, but soon these too died away in the distance, and it was in silence that they reached the hill-top. Anna's uncle said to her :

' It gives me a lump in my throat to hear them singing —there's a good many won't sing much longer.'

From the crest of the hill they could see the lighthouse where the River Vilaine entered the sea. On the horizon Anna saw a white glimmer which she fancied was a ship in full sail.

Shortly afterwards a furze hedge hid the one light which man had made in that wide darkness. Near the

Grand Néant, at the sight of his own land Jean-Guillaume went more slowly. Pointing to his fields, of grass and cabbages, he began to speak of Gildas :

' Before he went, Gildas gave me some useful advice about the farm. D'you think, Anna, that he is able to manage a farm ? '

' I'm sure he is,' she replied, ' especially with you to see that he doesn't make mistakes.'

In bed she asked herself why he had talked to her of Gildas—her uncle was not the man to talk for the sake of talking. There must be some reason for his remarks.

Three weeks later towards the middle of September a letter from Lorraine came to Penmur. Like most letters from the front it was short. It spoke of the dead Pol and made enquiries for all at home, but it told very little of the war. There was one passage, however, that none of them could forget. Not once but many times it was read aloud to the family as they sat in the lamplight : ' When reinforcements are needed, we shall be sent, but only God knows to what part. I don't mind. It'll be men and not targets that I'll aim at then. No more throwing bombs at imaginary enemies. I shall try to be worthy of you all.'

Soon Anna knew the words by heart ; for she repeated them to herself as with a troubled soul she went about her work on the farm.

Two days later Anna, this time alone, went to one of the last threshings of that harvest at a nearby farm. As before, after supper when the long day's work was done, the young people danced. She, having no heart to dance, offered to help the farmer's wife. When they had cleared the long tables and set the room in order, the last of the minuets and polkas and round dances was over.

Since they were going her way, Anna could not refuse to join the crowd of Muzillac girls. They went in a body with a band of young men before and another behind them. A pock-marked cripple who was exempt from military service led the company, playing so haltingly on his accordion that it too might have been lame.

One of the girls called to him : ' Prosper, sing " I love my wife." '

At once there were cries of : ' No—not that ! Sing " A suitor I am come." '

He sang the first two lines. The whole company joined in on the third, marching in time with it.

A suitor I am come, am come, am come ;
A suitor I am come
To ask your hand
In marriage.

You cannot have my heart, my heart, my heart ;
You cannot have my heart ;
For it is
With another.

I'll take my sword and kill him, and kill him, and kill him ;
I'll take my sword and kill him,
And I will have
Your heart.

If you take your sword and kill him, and kill him, and kill him,
I'll turn myself into an eel,
And you won't have
My heart.

If you turn yourself into an eel, into an eel, into an eel,
I'll come and fish beneath your rock,
And I will have
Your heart.

If you become a fisherman, a fisherman, a fisherman,
I'll turn myself into a rose,
And you won't have
My heart.

If you turn yourself into a rose, into a rose, into a rose,
I'll come and pluck you from your bush,
And I will have
Your heart.

If you pluck me from my bush, my bush, my bush,
I'll go into a convent,
And you won't have
My heart.

If you go into a convent, a convent, a convent,
I'll hear the sins which you confess,
And I will have
Your heart.

If you are my confessor, confessor, confessor,
I'll turn myself into a star,
And you won't have
My heart.

As in the Provençal version, the *lover* ends with this
challenge to which there is no response :

If you turn yourself into a star, into a star, into a star,
I'll be an angel up in heaven,
And as I said, I'll have
Your heart.

The song died away across the meadows and over
the moor. Anna had sung the first two lines.
During the rest of the song she walked in silence.
Guessing the reason, the others joined hands, making
her a prisoner. They were now outside the Penmur
gate.

' I must go,' Anna said. ' Good-bye, everybody.'

The accordion-player, a merry-hearted fellow despite
his lameness, like the others took her hand. He winked
at her :

' Had any news of Gildas, my dear ? If you haven't,
I have.'

They all laughed. The cripple went on: 'A pal
of mine saw him in Lorraine. He was ever so well
and he said " Remember me to all my folks and to
Anna ! " '

' Yes, we know ! ' said some of them. ' But is that
just a yarn ? '

A Muzillac girl curtsied, and said : ' Congratulations,
Anna ! It's a pity he's not here now. *He* should have
sung " I will have your heart " to you.'

Anna, who was twenty-two and older than most of
them, said with affected condescension : ' Prosper can't
help it. But you others should know better than to
sing round here. You ought to remember they've lost
Pol and the other boy's leaving Lorraine for the firing-
line.'

As Anna crossed the moor to the farm, she heard no
more singing from the little band of threshers on their
homeward way.

Her aunt was still up. It was her custom to see that
all her household were within doors and every bolt and
lock made fast, before she herself lay down to sleep.

Taking a candle, she said softly : ' While you were at the threshing, I've boiled the clothes. Armandine's been helping me. Finish them down at the pool in the morning.'

CHAPTER VII

PENMUR POOL

AUTUMN, like death, is slow of foot, and steals imperceptibly on. As the rye and the wheat have yellowed before them, so on the trees the first leaves turn from green to gold, though the sap may still run strong. When the sun is high the air has the sparkle and warmth of summer, but the early hours are damp and harsh with fog.

It was in such a fog that Anna Maguern, washing stick in one hand and small coffee-pot in the other, took the steep path down towards Penmur Pool, with Ange pushing his new barrow beside her full of a large bundle of clothes to be washed.

They left the farm buildings and, following the line of the cliff, took a winding path through an ancient gap in the rocks. This became a ledge of narrow and unequal rock that wandered down through bushes and brambles to the pool twenty feet below. Before they reached its far end, it had needed all the strength of the seventeen-year-old boy, strong though he was, to hold back the heavy barrow. On the dried mud of the bank among the trampled rushes he let fall the handles. Stretching his tired arms he said with a laugh : ' Well, it's all come down in one journey, but I'll have to make several to get it up again.' Stooping, he picked up the barrow, and followed Anna round the bend at the bottom of the cliff. Eventually their path brought them out to the fringe of the marsh, while the steep escarpment upon which Penmur stood was left behind, and before them was the glitter of the pool and of the river beyond. The strip of muddy beach before the cliff left at this time of year by the low water was so narrow that they had to walk in single file. They settled for the morning's work in the shelter of a jutting rock. Ange emptied the washing on a long flat stone suitable for their purpose. Glad to be rid of his burden, with swinging arms and a light step the boy left Anna kneeling there with the water lapping the stone at her feet.

At seven o'clock on this September morning the fog, hanging thick over the pool, hid other rocks that were also spread with linen. Into their rugged basin the several streams which fed Penmur Pool splashed and swirled. In front of her Anna could see only a stretch of water, with wreaths of fog now scattering in the light wind, and now driven before it, surrounding the girl and touching the cliff-wall behind her.

She began to wash : the linen was dipped, soaked, wrung, beaten white with the stick, quickly folded and stacked in the barrow. She washed steadily, scarcely raising her eyes from her work. The fog began to melt under the sun. Fantastic caverns, seen for a moment, at the next were gone ; stately castles rose and then were ruined ; at last like a broken host the main body of the fog began to retreat across the clear water. Through the thinning mists the sun appeared, pale as the moon at first and then slowly reddening. Suddenly the haze was pierced, and the middle of the lake shone with gleaming light. Tatters of fog, lit from below by the water, rose slowly to be caught by the wind and driven towards Billiers beach. The full stretch of Penmur Pool was now revealed. Anna looked over the reeds, past the golden light in mid-stream to the water-lilies by the farther bank. Beyond, she saw the steep cliff with the black strata of its rocks, with its narrow ledges and their broom bushes, and lastly the beginning of its wooded plateau where there was neither house nor any other sign of man's handiwork. Yet at no great distance behind the cliff, Anna knew, the daily life of two farms went busily on. Tired of the silence around her and rejoicing in the dazzle of the sun, with sudden jubilation she waved the washing-stick above her head and shouted at the full pitch of her voice: ' Hullo there, you Labrissot folk ! Hullo, you Kerligan folk ! '

This was sheer whimsicality ; for she knew that only the echo would answer her. Yet it was sufficient to send her back to her washing with a glad heart. For some reason the sunlight made her thoughts turn to Gildas, and she murmured to herself: ' He hasn't changed though he's at the war and so far off ; for he always mentions me when he writes. He isn't the kind who's always talking and trying to please everybody at once. Perhaps he'll be back in three months—or anyway in six. Why, after all these years I don't really know him— out there they'll scarcely know him at all. I'm sure that there isn't a more reserved and thoughtful boy than cousin Gildas in all the parish. That's not to say he hasn't a heart. It doesn't take much to grieve him—or to please him for that matter. But he keeps such a still tongue in his head that even his family often doesn't know what he's thinking. I'm sure he thinks a lot about us, and remembers me every day in his prayers . . . it must be nine months ago since he talked to me about being a priest . . . he's got over that, I expect—anyway, he will have by the time he gets back. Let me see, I'm nearly twenty-three—that means he's now twenty-one. How the time drags ! No one says the war will soon be over.'

As she washed, her thoughts ran on : ' Yesterday when they teased me about Gildas, I'm sure my face gave me away. They all know about him and me, though heaven knows I never told a soul. As soon as he gets back, they'll be on to him to ask him if it's true about us. Still, I expect he'll take it in good part. I'm in love enough, anyway. . . .'

At the thought she beat the linen on the slab with such violence that a teal, which until then had floated placidly in the middle of the pool, started up with whirring wings and disappeared towards the north. Anna, thinking of the love songs and ballads which she had heard or had sung at wedding feasts, watched it for a while and murmured : ' How I wish you could fly to him ! '

She laughed at the thought : suddenly the laughter died from her face. For a moment forgetful of the wet linen, she got to her feet and gazed northward over the pool after the disappearing bird.

' Even if you flew to the front,' she muttered, ' would you find him there ? Pol is dead and thousands like him, and we only get the news long after.'

For a while she worked in sad silence. Yet with youth sorrow goes as quickly as it comes. The sun fell warm on the pool, upon its withered reeds, upon its banks with their ridges of hard mud and upon the dank grass of the marshland. The air was loud with unseen larks. Through the splendour of the sunlight the burden of their song came to the good folk of Labrissot, of Kerligan and of Penmur, as it came to the girl whose heart echoed it : ' The day has begun with beauty ; it shall end with loveliness. God has made the earth miraculous with light. Seen from our high place, the earth is fair indeed. Let your hearts soar to heaven, as our wings are soaring now—for we are at heaven's gate. Till our singing ends, summer shall not finish.'

As Anna listened to the song of the larks, her eyes were full of dreams and her hands gentle as she worked :

' When Gildas comes home on leave, I shall wear my velvet dress !

' When Gildas comes, I shall make the pancakes that he loves !

' When Gildas comes, I shall gather gilliflowers ; for they are in bloom till after the frosts begin.

' When Gildas comes, I shall go to the end of the moor to be the first to greet him.'

At noon when Ange returned, he found her still at work. The barrow was piled high with the sweet clean linen. ' You'll make a good housewife, Anna,' her cousin said.

' That's what I've been thinking,' she replied with a laugh.

The boy half unpacked the barrow, and with this lighter load climbed the path to the farm. On his return he found a tired and happy Anna seated on a stone, watching the sparkling water. Together they went back to Penmur.

CHAPTER VIII

TOLD IN CONFIDENCE

On November 11, 1916, a letter from Gildas dated from the Front two days previously reached Penmur. It ran :

' I have shifted since I wrote. We finished our training at the end of October, and changed camp. Our first move was to Villers-Bretonneux—I'm supposed not to mention names, but they will be safe with you. Several others and myself got orders to rejoin the 135th, our old regiment. When we reached it at Morlancourt on November 6, we found it resting. It would seem a queer kind of resting to you who are used to the quiet nights at the farm. Often a soldier's rest is about as unrestful as it can be. At eleven o'clock that first night a terrifying din began outside. We woke to find the earth shaking. We sleep in our clothes, and so, rushing out to see, it did not take us many seconds to discover what the first explosion had been. There was a great glare in the sky, and we found out afterwards that it came from Cerisy-Gailly, two and a half miles away from here. German air-raiders had blown up the munition dump there, and were now circling over our camp. We were not allowed to light a cigarette, which might have warmed us up a little, and goodness knows we needed it, as there wasn't a scrap of glass left in the windows of our billets.

' The force of the explosion had smashed the stained-glass windows of the church—it was already badly shattered. Our men had gone to service earlier in the evening—just the Rosary, an instruction, and Benediction. I had a good look at the chaplain. We are going to find that he is the man for his work, I think. He looks plucky as well as good. We shall need all our pluck soon. For any day now we expect to go up the line to relieve the boys. Mention them and us when you have prayers, won't you ?

' I'm keeping very well. But it's much colder here than at home. The rain comes down in buckets. If Penmur Pool got half of it, it would take a short cut to the sea by flooding the Vannes road.'

Gildas was not mistaken. On November 10 he went into the trenches. During the night the regiment passed by Marlicourt, Maurepas, and Combles. Further on, a sign-board on the one building left with some semblance of its old shape told the advancing column that here had once stood the village of Frégicourt. It had been demolished only a few days before ; the men threw scraps of ration bread to a cat that mewed among the ruins.

The 135th made a small part only of the long column which with its lorries, cars, and big guns marched through labour corps parties waiting to go on remaking the road when the column had passed. Ahead, at a distance impossible to guess in the darkness, flashes shone in the sky and died away, while on all sides were explosions followed by livid glares. On three occasions shells burst in the adjoining fields and once on the road itself. There were cries in the darkness as the men first stopped and then scattered across the open country. After an

interval the march was resumed, the men closing their
ranks to file by the dead and dying left where the shell
had burst. At times they found themselves in the sodden
fields, slippery under foot; in the shell-holes a man
would slide at intervals and the last they saw of him was
a waving arm.

When the men of the relief party took over from
those in the trenches, they were exhausted with marching, dripping with sweat despite the cold night air and
caked with mud that weighted down their cloaks.
Though it was two o'clock in the morning, they at once
set to work with pick-axe and spade. The French had
had no time to consolidate the ground which they had
taken on the previous day. Consequently there were
neither trenches nor dug-outs. The front line men
handed over a mere string of shell-holes to the relief.
These the 135th linked together by a shallow ditch rather
than a definite trench. Fear that day would come too
soon made them work faster. The muscular ploughmen
from Mauge, Saumur, Craonne, and Bauge were more
effective at this trench-digging than their less practised
comrades. Bullets came whistling from the nearby
German lines and caused a few casualties. As the mud
scattered about them with soft thuds, the soldiers
laughed and joked : ' The boys didn't leave the house
very straight, did they ? And it will take at least two
days to clear up after them.'

When day broke bitterly cold, the men were behind
their improvised shelters, some lying outstretched
asleep on their shovels, others peering from the cover of
clods of earth and trying to calculate the danger of their
position. Their trenches ran in a serrated line whose
nearest points were within twenty-five yards of the

Germans. Around them was the wide and undulating plain of Morval with its fields of mangolds and its gentle slopes and shallow valleys, left waste and overgrown with thistles for at least two years past. Here and there on the slopes were little spinneys, most of whose trees were felled : their levelling had not been the work of wood-cutters but of the French and German guns. Everywhere paths had been torn through the undergrowth, leaving it brown and devastated ; after twelve months of withered saplessness, broken and blasted oaks stood gaunt and smudged black as charcoal. In all that vast plain there was not a tree left whole. The very bushes had been pounded and flattened that they might offer no cover to advancing troops. The last traces of vegetation had been swept from the now naked soil. The one shadow was thrown by the crest of the small hills when the slanting sunlight fell upon them.

During the night of the 14th word reached the men that a party of the 135th was to attack a German post situated on a slight slope opposite their section of the line. Their orders were to take prisoners so that the German units holding that particular sector might be identified. For two hours the French artillery bombarded the fort. In their trench shelter Gildas Maguern and a crowd of others waited for the zero hour which they neither longed for nor dreaded. The attack was a necessity : they would make the attack. If their bodies flinched, their souls stood firm. A few made a pretence at sleep lest their fear should be read in their eyes—genuine sleep was made impossible by the noise of the guns. Breathing was not easy ; for the air was stale in the crowded shelter. Trickles of water from the deluge of the day before soaked through the branches and wooden beams overhead.

Their sole light came from an electric torch that the sergeant covered with a protecting hand, so that its brightness fell full upon his own face. Seated by his side, Gildas confirmed his first impression that he was young and fair and clean-shaven, with the face of a choir-boy and the phlegm of a philosopher.

The sergeant drew his watch from the big pocket of his cloak, looked at it and put it back. When shells burst very near to him, he gave an involuntary start, knocking his head against the dug-out wall. His lips moved as though in prayer. He had only to stir for every man's eyes to be swivelled upon him.

The bombardment grew more intense. A runner came panting in ; two sentries were killed. The dark disc of sky which ended the trench joining the dug-out turned a glimmering grey. The minutes went by. A quarter-past six—twenty past six—twenty-five past six. At half-past six the sergeant sprang up and said in an unhurried yet incisive voice : ' Forward, Section ! Follow me, boys ! '

They started to their feet ; they pushed and jostled in the narrow trench ; they climbed into the field beyond it and began to run up the slope towards the enemy post some thirty yards distant. Several were cut down much as the corn growing in that same field had been cut down two years before.

The rest of the men reached the enemy lines, killing three and capturing two others who had thrown down their arms. Gildas was the second to leap down into the trench. A bomb fell at his feet. Before it could explode, he had hurled it over the parapet. At the point of his bayonet he drove before him the German who had thrown it, making for the shell-holes and trench-shelter of the 135th. The earth spattered about them as thickly as straws from a flail.

Suddenly, giving his prisoner into the charge of a comrade, he swerved to the right and gained a slight hollow in which two men were kneeling by the side of the prone body of a third. For he had recognised in the two who knelt the chaplain and a stretcher-bearer, and in the dying man at their feet the sergeant of his half-section. The sight of that boyish face had made it impossible for Gildas to go on : he offered to take the other in.

As he made his offer, the sergeant muttered : ' Oh, this pain ! It's all up with me. You go. Get clear yourselves ! '

His abdomen was ripped open. Blood soaked through his uniform into the earth. His bleeding intestines hung through the gaping wound : the chaplain endeavoured to put them back by wrapping his cloak tight round the sergeant's body and buttoning it close. The man screamed in agony. Machine-gun bullets pinged about them. The chaplain said : ' All right, my poor chap, all right ! They've come to fetch you in.' Noticing Gildas for the first time, he added curtly : ' What are you doing here ? This spot isn't healthy. Two of us are quite enough for this job. Clear off with you ! '

Gildas obeyed. Both he and the two men, who a moment later followed him with the wounded man between them, reached the trench in safety. But the sergeant died. On the next night he was buried in a fallow field. The chaplain said the burial service and afterwards made a cross with a couple of sticks. The men loved him ; for in him they saw a comrade who fought with them and for them, using spiritual where they used material weapons. Gildas had a specially keen sense of this comradeship. When he saw the chaplain leave, he told himself that the two of them would certainly meet again.

They did meet again, but not at once. From November 15 to 20 heavy rain continued to fall. In spite of this rain and the severe cold which followed it, the frozen soil had to be dug and trenches made to replace the others, which were no more than ditches. Bronchitis, frost-bite and bullet-wounds accounted for many casualties among the 135th. On the night of the 20th, after eleven days in this exposed and vulnerable sector, the survivors were relieved. Gildas was one of those who, neither wounded nor sick, marched past General Fayolle. This tall slim soldier was wrathful at the length of time the men had been left in so dangerous a position. He ordered them to be sent at once to a rest camp in the far rear.

Their first move was to Corbie. From Corbie they went to Cerisy-Gailly, which had been left half in ruins by the explosion of November 6. Gildas and four of his chums who had found a cellar, some straw, and an iron bedstead congratulated themselves on a luxurious billet. Twelve miles behind the line, the village was bombed from the air almost nightly, while from it the course of each day's fighting could be followed by the ear if not by the eye, as artillery duels were succeeded to the north or the south by surprise sorties, big offensives, or skirmishes.

Here they were at peace, or almost at peace. Supplies were abundant and food was served hot—the trenches

seemed in another world. After drill the men smoked
or drank, strolled or slept. A few spent their time
otherwise. This interlude between danger past and
danger yet to come set them thinking of old forgotten
things and of old familiar faces. Some said their
prayers. With the approach of Christmas memories of
Midnight Mass came to many ; they had visions of their
families in procession through the winding lanes and deep
country roads. Gildas Maguern pictured himself at the
stable door in Penmur yard harnessing Bounce and
seeing how bright her eyes were. Once again he saw
his brothers, his sisters, and Anna with her velvet
apron.

Two days before Christmas, when five o'clock brought
the early winter darkness, men came pouring out of all
the cellars, barns and sheds still intact in Cerisy-Gailly.
They made their way towards the shattered and tottering
church. Inside the building the air was bitterly cold,
while rain dripped through the roof and drove through
the gaping windows which the explosion had stripped of
their glass.

The men flocked to the choir where the chaplain was
hearing confessions. He was in his cassock, seated at the
far end near the altar on a form that had only three legs,
an upturned chair supplying the fourth. Stretched in
front of him was a strip of carpet upon which the
penitents knelt. A candle in a former processional
lantern set upon a choir stall provided the one poor light.
Faces could not be distinguished ; they could only be
guessed at. The men were there in such numbers that
those waiting, seated or standing or kneeling where they
could find room, jostled the man making confession.
' Not so loud ! They'll hear you ! ' the chaplain would

say from time to time. Almost invariably the reply would come : ' There's no disgrace in confessing. Besides, I wasn't listening to the others when I was waiting.'

Gildas had to wait a full half-hour before his own turn came. Crossing himself he knelt on the carpet. It did not need many questions for the priest to recognise in him a pure and upright spirit. In the glimmering light to which his eyes had grown accustomed he admired the boy's frank face, even as he respected the ease and firmness of his answers and was moved by the straight gaze of his eyes. Sudden inspiration moved him to ask :

' What work do you do ? '

' I'm on the land.'

' So were my folks. Farming's a fine calling. Have you ever wanted to do anything else ? '

' Yes.'

' I'll wager that you've had the idea of being a priest ! '

' That's true. But I didn't want to talk about it to you now. The others might hear ! '

' Come along to-morrow after Mass, if you can. I shall be in the sacristy.'

The priest indicated with a gesture the door of the little room in which the church furniture had been kept in the past.

On the following day Gildas was able to keep his appointment. The chaplain welcomed him in with a friendly smile and a warm handshake. They found seats on the wooden steps before the ransacked sacristy cupboards.

' You don't remember me, do you, chaplain ? ' Gildas began.

' I think I do. I saw you yesterday, didn't I ? '

' You saw me at Morlancourt, too. You ticked me off
when I wanted to give a hand with the sergeant after
the attack.'

' So I did ! Now about yourself. You come from
Brittany, don't you ? '

' Yes, I'm a Maguern ; Maguerns are mostly Bretons ! '

' Well, my boy, what gave you the idea of wanting to be
a priest ? '

' It was queer you should ask me about it yesterday.'

' Queer ? Say one of God's mysteries ! Tell me all
you can ! '

The soldier turned towards the priest, but he looked
beyond rather than at him. He looked at the shattered
window and the free sky outside. He saw the one plum
tree and the three pear trees in a garden that buildings
had hidden till the explosion and bombardment had
left them a heap of ruins.

' There isn't much to tell. I was ten when it happened.
I was religious but I wasn't always thinking of God. I
certainly wasn't thinking of him that summer day. I
remember I had been to communion that morning.
I was standing in the hayloft with my pitchfork in my
hand when I heard the Voice say : " You shall be my
priest." I was full of joy ; my heart seemed to swell
inside me—oh, I can't tell you how glad I felt, Father !
It didn't cross my mind to answer ; I just listened and
felt happy. The Voice didn't say any more. When I
came to myself I found that I was changed. Till then
I'd thought of priests as a poor man thinks of a rich one.
I saw that men looked up to them, but they didn't seem
the same as ordinary men. It was different after that
day. I felt myself to be of the same flesh and blood.'

' Did you tell anyone what had happened to you ? '

' It worried me a lot. My parents were poor at that time. They're poor again now the war's on, because of the neighbours they have to help. I didn't tell my father because he's wrapped up in the farm and has so much to do and so few to help him do it. I said a word to my mother, though I asked her to keep it private. I saw she was pleased to think that one day I might be a priest, and she might hear me say Mass. The idea faded gradually. It was beginning to come back when a girl who's a relative of ours showed she liked me well enough to marry me. I told her that I had the idea of being a priest. She laughed, and I don't wonder ; it seems so foolish to want to be a priest when a man's my age and on the point of being called up——'

He looked down at his uniform, his knapsack, and his shoes with their caked mud.

' And you still want to be a priest ? '

' More than ever lately, since I've been in the army. I've never thought so much about it. Especially sometimes, of course. You remember November 14 when we made the surprise attack ? '

' I don't follow.'

' I mean what the sergeant said when he was lying wounded, and you were on your knees beside him. . . .'

' So it was you who came running up ? And I shouted : " Clear off with you ! This spot isn't healthy, and two's enough " ? '

' Yes.'

' You couldn't have heard what he said ! '

' The stretcher-bearer told me. That night I didn't get an hour's sleep for thinking of what he'd said.'

' Let's have it, my boy ! I'd like to know what that poor fellow said before I carried his dead body back to the shelter—the stretcher-bearer may have made it up.'

' No one could make up a thing like that ; it's much too fine. The sergeant's belly had been ripped open by a shell splinter. His blood streamed out—on the ground, over him, over you . . . ! '

' My cassock is still stained with it.'

' It was horrible. I couldn't bear to look at his bowels. You tried to force them back by buttoning his cloak round him. . . . It wasn't so much your order that made me go, but I could see he was already dying. His breath was getting faint, but he managed to say : " I'm in agony . . . but I'm ready to die, chaplain. I'm ready to die because I have brothers who are priests." '

The Father had grown pale as he remembered the horror of that morning. He nodded. ' Yes, it's true. He did say that ! '

He leaned forward, anxious to hear the rest. He was curious to know if the full story had reached the men in the trenches. The nod gave Gildas courage. He went on, looking full into the priest's eyes.

' Last of all he said to you : " But for the war I should have been ordained. How I'd longed for my ordination day ! But it wasn't God's will. . . ." His voice was too faint for you to hear, so both you and the stretcher-bearer bent over him. The shells whistled round you, but you heard him above the racket : " I did wrong to say that, chaplain. God himself ordained me just now. At this very moment I am saying my first Mass. With this blood of mine, just as Christ did."

'Five of us were told what he had said, back there in the trenches. I couldn't get the words out of my head. It seemed as if they had been said for my special benefit. . . .'

The chaplain took both of Gildas' hands and held them in his own. In silence he prayed for the farmer's son. There was a knock at the door. Gildas said hurriedly :

'Just a minute, chaplain. You don't think it silly of me to want to be a priest, do you ? '

'Time will prove, my boy. Think about it yourself, and I'll think about it for you.'

'I'll remember. But do you think it's possible ? '

'That depends on you. If you stick to the idea, and have pluck, you'll manage it.'

'I've no money ! '

'No need to worry about that.'

'I've never studied, and at my age it's not easy to start.'

'That's true ! It won't be easy. But you've often broken up clods of earth—well this will just be one more ! I'll give you a hand ! When I see how you shape, we'll start Latin together.'

'Where ? '

'Here.'

The men who had knocked came into the sacristy. With a gesture Gildas drove them out. Again he leaned towards the chaplain. His face wore that expression of white tense joy which it had worn on that other day in the hayloft.

'That'll need a miracle. . . . I'll come to see you again. . . . It's my belief I shan't be killed, so that . . .'

Leaving his remark unfinished, he went out.

During that day the news came that at two in the following morning the regiment was to start for Bouchavesnes, where reinforcements were needed. As on the previous day the church was crowded. The chaplain spoke encouragingly to the men.

' My friends, at midnight Christmas begins. We're under orders to move. But if you come along between twelve and two in the morning you'll still have time to hear Mass and receive Communion. Come along, and get your comrades to come too. Even those in the furthest billets needn't stay away. But they mustn't show a light when they cross the fields because of aeroplanes. . . . Come along all of you. For some it may be your last Christmas ! '

Two months went by. The regiment was resting once more, this time at Soulange in the Marne hill country. Sitting in the shade of a pine tree on the slope of a hill the chaplain gave Gildas his first lesson in Latin. Fine March days had brought a foretaste of summer, though the air was keener, and the grass more freshly green. As they sat, they could hear the distant rumble of the guns. On the slope of the hill beneath them an old man encouraged a weary horse that came to frequent halts along the brown furrows between the rows of vine plants. The Father opened a text-book and said :

' Latin's a queer language, you'll find. Every word has a lot of different forms according to its use. This grammar will teach you that. Take it away with you, will you ? '

From that March day onwards Gildas crammed into his knapsack pencil, note-book, and small Latin grammar. His comrades saw him reading in his leisure time. They were not concerned, for his secret was unknown to them. Equally it was unknown to those at Penmur farm, but the time when he must tell them was at hand.

CHAPTER IX

A DISCUSSION AT MME VOILIER'S

ALL Gildas' letters home, whether from the trenches or from the rest camps, had been short and so impersonal that they could have been as fittingly signed by one of his comrades. He was neither wounded nor gassed—this accounted for a line or so ; the weather had been good, bad or indifferent—this filled a couple of lines more ; they were far off but he had not forgotten them. This was almost all that Gildas wrote. Not quite all, because he seldom omitted to ask for news of the farm : did such and such a field still bear the best corn ; did his ' little brother ' still have luck with the fishing which he did on the quiet in the pool ; how were the young oxen shaping now that they were put to work, and how were the old ones faring,whom he called by their names as he had so often done in the fields ?

Jean-Guillaume, no great lover of reading, left his wife to take her old-fashioned glasses and read the boy's latest letter. When she had finished reading it aloud, he asked her to repeat those passages that dealt with the farm. ' He's a farmer born,' the old man would say. ' Don't forget to tell him so and so. He'll be interested.'

It was rarely that Gildas omitted some reference to or remembrance of ' my cousin Anna.' Either custom or courtesy dictated most of these references, yet Anna read into the few poor words that he wrote all the tenderness which she had stored in her dreamy heart as she went busily about her daily work. She imagined this tenderness—the words themselves did not express it or justify her own reflection that very soon after his return the church bells would ring for the two of them.

Only one member of the family had any great knowledge of Gildas' essential character. His mother alone knew that he was the kind of man who for years could cherish a secret dream and then put it from him because of a nobler ideal.

In this he was a true Breton. Many men of his race have heard the call of the sea and of the ' far strands ' of which they had been told in the fire-lit farm kitchens, and have left their homes, parents, and friends to follow that call and to sail those waters. Many others in an earlier day had forsaken their ancient Armorica and beyond its borders had sought out one of the famous monasteries of Greater Britain, where they might satisfy their souls' need and serve the glory of God, as had hundreds of their Celtic Christian forbears. In his boyhood just such a call had come to Gildas, but then the call to the Muzillac farmer's son had been as uncertain as now it was clear.

One Sunday morning a further letter marked *Army Post* and addressed to Mme Marie Maguern was collected in Muzillac by the farmer's wife who had gone there for high Mass. She was unwilling that any but herself should unseal her son's letters, but on this particular morning she had forgotten her horn spectacles, and she did not open the letter, which she carried first in her prayer-book and then in her hand that her fingers might caress it.

It was almost noon when she reached the farm. Alexis and Armandine were by the shed at the bottom of the yard sheltering from the sun, which on this hot windless March day made a shining dazzle of Penmur Pool. Their mother went into the living-room ; glanced at the saucepan bubbling on the fire ; inspected the box-beds, drawing the curtains of one of them ; and put the missal and rosary in the niche in her room which she called her chapel. As she returned to the main room she said to Denise and Jean-Guillaume who at that moment came in : ' I've got another letter from Gildas.'

Both watched her as she sat at the top of the table, using a knife to slit the envelope. Anna, who had come in with them, stopped short on the doorstep, leaning against the worn stones of the porch. From here she heard the old woman's clear voice as she lovingly read the words written by her son.

' " DEAR MOTHER,

" I am as fit as ever. If I hadn't had proof here in the Army that God wants me for another service, I should have thought myself born to be a soldier. You will remember when I was quite small that I told you what happened to me one day when I was working alone. I had a queer sort of joy in my heart, and the wish to be a priest and the feeling that one day I should become one. . . ." '

Marie Maguern stopped, and looking towards her husband, said :

' I said nothing of this to you, Jean-Guillaume, because the boy asked me not to. But it's true enough.'

She went on with her reading : ' " At that time we did not pay as much attention as we ought to have done to this sign from on high. You may remember that the only person except you that I told about it advised me to wait for a time, as father had to work so hard to bring us all up, and I was beginning to help him.

" Years went by, and father had more and more to do. Yet I never quite forgot my wanting to be a priest. Several times when I had to decide about my future I remembered it. It was only when I got into the Army and mixed with all the different types that my old idea came back to me. One day I will tell you how I came to talk about it to a chaplain who is very brave and much liked by the boys. When I first spoke I had no idea that at my age I could start to study. He told me I was wrong about this, and kept his eye on me for a good while. Now I am learning Latin with him, either in the trenches between attacks, or in rest camp behind the lines.

" Mother, please tell father that the chaplain says my studies need not cost a great deal—I might even get a scholarship . . . ! " '

' If the boy thinks I'm going to let him beg, I won't have it.'

' Don't interrupt, Jean-Guillaume. There's still half a page.'

. . . ' " I don't want to grieve him. I'm sure that my two brothers will work all the harder for him when they know they are taking my place, and when they remember that God has called me to do his work instead of the farm's.

" Tell my cousin Anna from me, will you please. . . . " '

Marie Maguern turned slightly to look at Anna. The girl still stood motionless on the threshold : her face was turned away—she appeared to be watching the scurrying clouds.

' " —that if I had married at all, she would have been my wife. But I am not to have a wife. The misery of the world is to be dear to me and that is all. Already this begins to be true.

" So far, mother dear, I have not had the leave which I might have had before I went into the trenches. If there is not too much fighting, it won't be too long before I see you all again. Perhaps in April or May, the captain says." '

The old woman finished her reading. She had reached the end of the letter except for the good-byes said to each member of the family. She had no sooner put down the written sheets when Jean-Guillaume, striking the table with his fist, said :

' We'll see about this ! Gildas is not going to leave Penmur, if I have to go to the trenches to have a talk with that chaplain he talks about.'

' You wouldn't have the chance, my dear.'

As Marie Maguern spoke, there was upon her face that look of resolution which it never wore except when she had suffered deep hurt. As though she would have obliterated the words he had spoken she raised her hand protestingly between herself and him, and went on :

' Jean-Guillaume, I'm surprised at you ! '

' What do you mean ? '

' You're trying to stop our boy from obeying God, who has called him.'

' What do you know about such things ? '

' Priests know if I don't. They make a study of them ! '

' They don't know what I'm up against, with three farms to manage, and two of them worked out of charity.'

' Gildas has already been away for fourteen months. Yet you've managed with Ange and Alexis ! '

' I can't much longer.'

' The war won't last much longer.'

Jean-Guillaume half turned, shaking his fist at someone or something unknown and saying :

' I'm against it, I tell you ! And I'm going to let him know it.'

' And I'm for it. It'll be an honour for Penmur.'

Jean-Guillaume shrugged his shoulders.

' You mean " ruin," ' he said, ' and my death, maybe.'

He strode straight to the door. He passed Anna without giving her a glance, and went towards the shed where the children were waiting in the sun for dinner-time. He said to Alexis :

' Run along in, and bring me a piece of bread and a slice of bacon. I shan't be in to dinner ! '

Marie Maguern went to Anna, who stood silent with hanging head and with tears streaming down her face and on to her dress.

' I know how you're feeling, Anna my dear. I understand. . . . You're in love with him . . . I'm sure of that from little things I've noticed. It's not Gildas who has given you up, but God who has taken him from you . . . and from us too. Here come the children, so dry your poor eyes. Later on we'll have a talk. . . . You're like a daughter to me, dear ! '

Denise had said nothing. When her father-in-law had said angrily that Gildas should never enter the seminary with his consent, it was plain to see that she had not sided with him in the matter. She was by no means reluctant that Gildas should become a priest, since he as eldest surviving son would then no longer be at the farm to deprive her of the authority which she held there.

Thus for very different reasons, from the moment when the letter was read in the living-room, two of those at the farm were willing that the Latin lessons should continue. They were resigned to the fact that from this time, an exile from his family, from Muzillac, and even from Brittany, he would seldom be seen in that room where they had talked of him.

Anna saw that with Marie Maguern at least the resignation came of self-sacrifice and love of God. With a troubled spirit the girl asked herself whether she had the right to rebel when the boy's mother was thus resigned, or to weep when the other rejoiced. God had gained what she had lost : was her rebellious love more to her than her Christian faith ?

While she attended to their needs at table and for an hour after the meal was finished, her grief was so plain and poignant that twice Armandine threw her arms about her and kissed her. When she had cleared and washed the dishes, she went to her aunt. Marie Maguern had just retired to her room, for on the days when she could not go to vespers, she was wont to read the psalms indoors. Anna said to her :

' If there's nothing more for me to do, I'll go to Muzillac. After church I'll very likely call on a friend.'

The old woman perceived that Anna had great need of a comforter—such a comforter as she herself could not be, at this hour when hope and joy and pride possessed her because of her son's letter. As she looked tenderly at Anna, she saw that the girl's eyes were dully miserable beneath the splendour of her almost queenly head-dress.

She saw too that there was no rancour mixed with the misery, but only a yearning to be understood. For it is a belief with the young that the old do not understand them.

' Go, by all means, my dear ! You're very wise to get away from here to-day. Denise and I will do what has to be done.'

Anna went her way to Muzillac. She was one of the first to leave the church. Hurrying that she might not be delayed in talk, she turned from the shops, and by narrow lanes reached the outskirts. She came to familiar fields and crossed them by tracks as familiar. It was mild and windless. Here and there fat buds were beginning to burst on the bramble bushes, and willow-catkins to hang beautiful on trees and hedgerows and near the banks of the little nameless streams. On that Sunday evening the peaceful fields where none sowed or tilled gave glory to God by their silence. Anna was not untouched by it. She found herself thinking : ' These are pleasant parts. If only we could have settled down here. . . . To be a priest is a fine thing, but so it is to be a husband and father.'

Already she had begun to say : ' If only we could have settled down here,' for her old hope was broken beneath the blow which that day had brought it.

Two partridges whirred upward from a young green wheatfield. Anna watched them cross the hedge, and fly into the adjoining fallow field. There they stayed together for a time, and in the end together disappeared.

Disregarding the thorns which grew on either side, whose prickles pierced her black frock and grey woollen shawl, Anna took the steep hill path as the shortest way to Coléno Farm. With its two high bramble-covered banks it made a kind of tunnel through which she groped along to the house on the hill.

She came upon it suddenly, perched with its sweeping roof and squat walls on the windy crest. On either side of the diminutive door were two small windows that looked towards the distant sea and were bright with the sun or beaten by the wind and rain as days were fair or stormy. There were no trees around its tiny square of garden, whose careful digging and planting and weeding were plain to see. Bordering the garden in place of trees were a few wooden stakes with iron wires between them. On both sides of the central gravel path were beds of young onions with their spear-like shoots, and parsley with its delicate green fronds, while beans, sown before their time, already stood high. At the end of the gravel path were great clumps of lavender. They had been planted many years before, and their immense round bushes, that on this March day were no more than faded grass stalks, would in the summer months to come be a massed purple loveliness scenting all the hill-side with its fragrance.

Beyond the lavender Marguerite Voilier sat in her high-backed chair with half-closed eyes, enjoying the air and her thoughts. Anna could have chosen no better confidante than this woman whose soul was both simple and wise—wise with the wisdom which comes of solitude and calm retrospection and poverty accepted with resignation.

When Anna had first gone to work at Penmur the widow had said to herself at their first meeting : ' There's a girl just made to be loved.' From that time they had exchanged pleasant words each time they met. Memories of these talks had led Anna to turn her steps unhesitatingly towards the small house on the highest crest of all the hilly Muzillac country. For in this old woman, living in want and alone, Anna had discovered a heart full of an exceeding tenderness, that could not turn her own heart empty away.

The widow had not heard Anna's slow steps on the gravel. As she sat there she looked old and tall and thin. The painful rheumatism from which she suffered had tinged her expression with severity. This was in part because her eyes were hidden. They were blue eyes, with a hint of violet in their blue—not unlike the lavender flowers which that summer would bring to blossom. Even the small school-children felt the charm of her eyes, and gave her friendly greeting when they passed.

It was hard to say why it was such pure pleasure to receive the glance of this simple-hearted woman. It had nothing to do with material things. When still very young Marguerite Voilier had become a farm servant. Her pay was as poor as her features were plain. At about thirty she had married a labourer from Guerno, the village next to her own. Three years later he had died, leaving her his debts and their one son.

The son was now in the Army, and with the same resolution he showed in the trenches, his mother held to Coléno, rising early and working late, yet even so dependent for her livelihood on the charity of Jean-Guillaume, who tilled her fields and in part harvested them. Yet the widow, unworldly wise as she was, had a soul that was rich in prayer and peace and good counsel both for herself and for others.

The widow was so deep in thought that Anna reached

her chair, stood beside it for a moment, and had to bend towards her before her eyelids fluttered open, and her face was lit with gentle welcome.

' So you've come to pay Coléno a visit at last, my dear ? I often see your uncle here, as he comes to help with the farm work now my son is away, but it isn't often I see you. But then you have to stay at home, don't you ? Have you brought a message ? '

' Oh no, I haven't been sent, Marguerite Voilier : it's on my own account I'm here ! '

The widow leaned towards the young girl, and seeing her sad face said :

' You're troubled about something, my dear ? '

' Yes, Marguerite.'

' Bring a chair from the living-room and come and sit here beside me. There's nobody to hear what we say. Young Jeannette who helps with the cows and in the house has gone to Muzillac, and won't be back till late. Bring the chair.'

Very soon the two were talking quietly, their four hands resting white and still upon their black dresses.

Before them the wide expanse of earth melted into the still wider sky. From their high vantage they looked upon a mosaic of fields and hedgerows dwindling in the distance until they melted on the horizon where lay the hidden sea. No wind blew over the quiet earth.

' Oh, Marguerite, I'm ill with worry.'

' Ah yes, we all know suffering early enough,' the widow answered. ' I've had plenty in my time, and very little else.'

' Well, I've had my happy days, but I believe they're over now.'

She began to tell the story of her love for Gildas : she spoke briefly of earlier days, but more fully of the time since her unhappy walk over the moor. Neither the younger woman who spoke, nor the elder who listened, looked at the other : they might almost have been figureheads on two ships moored side by side, so still they sat, looking out on the wide horizon.

When she came to those words which, heard only that morning, had come to have sorrow in their very sound, Anna's control forsook her, and with a hint of shrillness in her tones she half turned from the tranquil landscape to Marguerite Voilier.

' I want you to get it clear, so that you can advise me. You do see, don't you, after what I've said, that I can't marry anyone except Gildas Maguern ? He'll soon be home on leave. I can see him then if I want to, that's very sure. There's nothing to prevent me going by train to meet him outside the dome of S. Anne's, my patron saint. He'll be his own master for the ten days he's home on leave. I can talk it over with him then, and find out how he feels.'

The widow herself looked a little like a gaunt and meditative S. Anne as she answered :

' It's plain that you still have a hold over him. But take care, my dear.'

' Marguerite, I've been quite frank. I've kept nothing back. Ever since his letter came, I've been making and unmaking plans. I've gone over in my mind what we shall say to each other : it's been as real to me as if he talked to me and I answered him.'

' Tell me about your thoughts to-day.'

' I will. You're better able to judge than I. I'm suffering too much. Supposing I do meet him at the steps of S. Anne's church, like pilgrims making our vows, and supposing I whisper so that only he and God can hear. Dare I ask him if he can really hope to learn Latin from the chaplain out there at the front ? Or if he thinks he can ever become a priest ? Dare I say that perhaps it's all a mistake about this vocation, as it has been with many before. . . .'

' You can't do that ! For it would only worry him. Has he given you the right to talk to him on a matter like this ? Has he promised to marry you ? '

' No, Marguerite Voilier, don't mistake me : he hasn't promised. . . . It was his call that held him back. I remember once he was on the point of asking me, when again the call came to him. So perhaps I should say to him : " Don't let me stand in you way, Gildas : maybe I've loved you more than you've loved me. I don't blame you for that. . . ." '

The older woman turned to Anna. For the first time they looked at each other :

' You've actually said that to yourself ? '

' Yes.'

' Would you really be strong enough ? '

When Anna saw the growing admiration in Marguerite's eyes, she shook her head vigorously, and looking down to hide her anguish said :

' Oh, don't go on ! I can't bear to think of it for more than a minute. Our thoughts are like dogs that get loose. We've just got to keep control of them. Just now, Marguerite, the thought of telling him to go is agony to me. For then of my own accord I've thrown everything away. What will there be left for me ? I shall be as much a widow as you, without ever being a wife. . . . It's silly, though, to take any notice of these fancies of mine. The one thing certain is that he's coming home on leave. . . .'

' Yes, my dear. Perhaps he's already on the way.'

' Yes, perhaps he is. Can't I tell him what I really feel ? '

' No, Anna ! '

' I know that I shall cry as soon as I see him—all I'll be able to think of will be getting him back. . . . I see by your sad look that even you don't understand. I had hoped you would ! '

Once more she turned her head away to look out over the fields towards the mist-hidden sea. In her gentle voice the other said :

' What do they say at Penmur, my dear ? '

' They don't all think alike.'

' What does your uncle think ? '

' He's against Gildas, because he wants his help on the farm.'

' Your Aunt Marie ? '

' She's for Gildas—she sees him saying Mass later on.'

' What about Denise ? '

' I think she wants Gildas to be a priest, then she'll be surer of staying at the farm. Oh, Marguerite ! They think of him, or they think of themselves : none of them thinks of me. At least, to be fair, Aunt Marie has done, a little, perhaps.'

The widow, who had known much grief in her life, made no immediate reply. Once more the two women, sitting erect and still in their chairs, gazed pensively before them, over the now darkening fields. Night had fallen on the country-side and its villages. Only on the far horizon was the darkness streaked by a pale light that shone over the distant sea and its rocky shore, where the evening star would shortly shine. Though they said no word, both women took comfort at the sight of this distant glow. As they continued to gaze, they each found life a little sweeter. Marguerite Voilier said, rather as though she were a mother talking to her little one :

' My child, God alone has compassion. He knows all our sorrows. Think of him, not of yourself—then you will have his blessing. For you know there are some joys which at first we think are griefs, but later we learn to know for what they are.'

Anna got up to go, and went her way across the fields. By the path along which she had come, a girl climbed, humming, to the house she had left.

Seven o'clock was striking as Anna reached Penmur. It was already dark, and the sky was full of stars. She soon saw that they had been anxious about her, because of her late return. The baby Marie held out her arms to Anna, while Denise looked at her supper, which was laid out on the table, and her glance said plainly that she did not wish to do Anna's work again. The two Maguern boys, warming themselves at the inglenook, looked first at Anna, and then away from her. Their unspoken thought was : ' She'll get a good talking to ! Father's been out of temper ever since that letter came this morning ; we can hear him arguing with mother in their room. He's called for Anna twice, and she wasn't here. Yes, she'll catch it hot.'

As they were thinking thus, Jean-Guillaume opened the door and, seeing his niece, called to her :

' Come here, Anna. I want a word with you.'

His tones were more tender than the boys had ex-

pected. The old people had not lit candle or lamp, and
the bedroom was in almost total darkness. For it is not
necessary to see in order to argue. For an hour they
had wrangled, neither yielding to the other. In the
shaft of light from under the living-room door, Marie
Maguern could be seen in vague outline in a corner close
to the window. Her breath came quickly as she bent
forward, wiping her eyes with the handkerchief which
she clutched with both hands. Near her Jean-Guillaume
was standing. As soon as Anna had come quietly into the
room, he said, lowering his voice that the children should
not hear him :

' I've written to Gildas, Anna. The letter's posted.
He has the notion of becoming a priest, so he says now,
though before the war I never heard a word of it.'

' Well, I did ! ' his wife broke in, and once more sank
into dejected silence.

' It was wrong of you not to tell me, Marie ; and now
it's too late. Whoever heard of a boy past twenty going
to college, at least in this part of the world ? I've no
patience with a grown man who wants to change his
trade. If it's helping his fellow-men he's after, he can
do that here by helping me on the farm. His duty lies
here. I can't keep on much longer, and nor can you,
mother. We'll have to leave Penmur and settle down in
Muzillac, somewhere near the church.'

Touching Anna on the shoulder, he went on :

' Our niece here will look after the place gladly enough
for him. I said all that in my letter to Gildas, to-day,
and told him to give up these antics of his at once.'

The tired old woman rose. In the dark her eyes
glowed indignant at the hurt to her faith.

' For shame, Jean-Guillaume ! '

' I shall say what I choose.'

' Even a heathen wouldn't talk like that.'

' Maybe.'

' Even your brother Corentin wouldn't do what you're doing,' Marie Maguern made bold to say.

Jean-Guillaume laughed harshly. In his laughter resentment mingled with defiant anger. Again he glanced at his niece :

' Let her go and ask him, and you'll see ! '

As he groped his way to the door, once more his resentful laughter was heard by the children in the next room. They imagined this a sign of his restored good-humour. ' So much the better ! ' they thought. ' They've finished quarrelling.'

They were mistaken.

That night, after the boys had gone to their room, her aunt took Anna aside to talk near the hearth. She said :

' You didn't go to Monks' Island to see your father last year and you haven't been this. Surely it's time you paid him a visit ? You'd better not leave it much longer. As your uncle's said you may, perhaps you'd better go to-morrow.'

' All right, I'll go,' Anna answered her.

CHAPTER X

RETURN TO MONKS' ISLAND

EARLY next morning Ange drove Anna in the waggonette
to the station, where she caught the first train on the
Roche-Bernard-Vannes line. Tied in a white napkin
she carried was a change of linen ; three head-dresses
which she knew would be ironed better in the islands
than at Muzillac ; a pair of clogs to wear on the beach
near her father's house, and four pippins from the apple-
room that Marie Maguern had given her at the last
moment, saying :

'I was keeping them for Gildas, but give them to your
father : I'm sure he has none in Monks' Island.'

It is only a short journey from Muzillac to Vannes.
Anna reached the little capital of south Brittany before
the sun had warmed the chill March air. She had to
hurry, however, as the small steamboat started early.
As she walked briskly away from the station through
the keen air, she wondered why her Aunt Marie should
wish to consult her father about Gildas' vocation.

She found herself thinking : ' I didn't choose to come
home on this errand. My father has very little religion
left in him, and what he has is well hidden. It'll be
strange to be home again after all this time : father will
be pleased to see me, but when I ask him if my uncle
or my aunt is right about Gildas, he'll probably just

laugh at us all. Then to-morrow, after making a fuss of me, he'll very likely send me back, telling me to marry Gildas since he is better off than we are. It's precious little he knows about him, though ! There's no love lost between father and uncle—and it's not to be wondered at, either ! How shall I tell him that Aunt Marie has sent me on this errand, that means so much to her with her faith ? I suppose it was the only way she could hold out against her husband, poor woman ! '

She quickened her step ; for the steamboat's warning whistle had already blown. On board she made her way to the bows where women and girls with their market baskets were grouped. A priest had his breviary open before him. There were sailors going home on leave. A tradesman's family, father, mother, four children playing at ' runaway horses,' and a fifth asleep in its nurse's arms, were evidently going to some holiday villa on Monks' Island or Arradon or Port Navalo that was doubtless at that moment being swept and garnished for their stay.

Three small pigs, huddled against the bulwarks with their feet bound, squealed at intervals. The steamer's screw began to revolve : soon the water swirled from the prow and swept foaming towards the river's banks, where the reeds bent before it and the foreshore received its muddy waves.

From le Morbihan several boats came sailing towards them ; a motor-barge passed with a cow and her calf ; an old tub with two red sails drew near with some twenty women or girls aboard, each with a basket of fish at her feet. Some were fair and some dark : all wore the embroidered and diadem-like head-dress of the islands. Anna craned forward with eager emotion as the two

vessels passed each other within a dozen yards. One of
the girls excitedly pointed out Anna and flashed her
white teeth in animated talk. The distance between
the two ships increased : soon red sails and baskets and
women and the unknown girl who had smiled were left
far behind. The Vannes River widened. Villas crowded
down to the right bank, which they were hugging, with
trees behind them. Everywhere the first new leaves
were to be seen. It was a fine morning and the air had
become warmer. As they drew abreast of the islands,
the sea-breeze grew less keen. Soon le Morbihan came
in sight.

Anna stood in the bows, leaning on the rail above the
suspended anchor. All her heart went out at the sight
of this scattered panorama of islands delicately etched
upon the calm waters of the familiar gulf, and enclosed in
the sloping banks of the widening river as it flowed on to
the seaport of Locmariaquer, half-hidden in its sea-fogs
where broad river and wide ocean met. Anna gazed
with quiet delight at her own country wrapped in the
beauty of luminous mist. Because of the mussel-beds
which the tide barely covered, the sea's deep blue became
a paler blue about the beaches of the islands. Soft sunlight suffused this mist through which two shining blurs
showed white. Anna knew them at once as Cadouarn
in Sené parish and the village on the isle of Arz.

On the mainland every house is whitewashed, yet they
fail to dazzle as do the island homes. The whitest of
clouds is less white than these newly washed houses of
Arz and of Sené that are the delight of the retired
seamen who live in them. At the sight of them they
remember the sails of their ships. They recall the land-
marks by which they themselves once set their course,

and choose that their houses should set a course for others. Compared with their shining white the rest of the landscape is drab : the ploughed fields or the winding roads round le Morbihan, the velvet sheen of young wheat or the moors with their broom, the sand-banks, rocks, or trees on the river bank with their green dust of new buds and leaves. Anna, idly watching the shipping, noted this red sail or that black hull coasting the islets of Logoden, threading the channel between Bouëte and Arz, or heading for the open sea beyond Monks' Island. The days of her childhood came back to her as her heart recalled one by one these beloved names.

The steamer passed the harbour bar of the island of Arz. As Anna knew, they were now heading direct for the island that was her home, and now she forgot every-thing save that she was soon to see her father again. After two years' absence, in what state would she find the little farm where she had been born ? Her father did not expect her : she might well have to track him from one farm to another—from Kergrancie to Kerno, she told herself, knowing his haunts as she knew his habits ; for he was a man who spent as much time in the houses of others as in his own home.

From the steamer, now moving slowly against the strong current, could be seen the nearest point of the island, the long bay, the tiny port, and the diminutive jetty running out from a rocky headland, planted with pines and lambertianas.

Beyond the small boats and smacks anchored near the shore Anna could see the road which she would soon have to climb, winding upwards until it disappeared between houses and fruit-trees and orchard walls, towards the high northern ridge of the island. In fancy she climbed that road, crossing one end of the village and reaching her father's house on the eastern side. House after house, landmark after landmark, came back to her memory. She remembered what she thought she had forgotten utterly : schooldays and the years spent at home with her mother, who was then the most beautiful woman on the island.

Her mother had died young. Her death had not been the beginning of sorrow. Noémie Bohan had come of seafaring stock. Born in the village of Arzon, near Port-Navalo, she had known early that love of the sea which makes the thought of an inland home intolerable. It was not long after her marriage to Corentin that she persuaded him to leave his brother Jean-Guillaume and the fine farm in Muzillac for a few acres of land on the foreshore of Monks' Island. She had lived long enough to see Corentin ruined and to know that she had helped him to his ruin by her follies, by her love of dress and of outings, and by her fondness for the attentions of retired ships' captains and of boat-owners who took her for trips to feasts and to fairs. While she gadded to Auray or to Vannes, or even further down the Gulf to Houat and to Belle Île, her husband, left alone, spent on drink the small earnings of his badly-kept fields. Anna and the two boys had been left to run almost wild.

The girl had been fortunate. An old woman of the island had taught her and in a measure brought her up. In her piety she had taken pity on the child. Anna had passed her girlhood days knowing few caresses and little of a mother's tenderness. The growing child's chief interest had been in her soul and in what the future might hold.

The steamer reached the jetty, most of the passengers disembarked, among them Anna, with her white package under her arm. Sudden regret and apprehension filled her heart ; for she had surely undertaken this journey with too little thought. It would serve no useful purpose. It might even prove to be disastrous for herself. What if her father tried to keep her ? He might well beg her to stay at the farm to look after him and to work in place of her brothers who had gone to sea. Did she refuse, he would grow angry and by his tirades set the neighbours against her as an undutiful daughter.

The score or so of passengers whom she followed up the cobbled street dwindled to a dozen and then to fewer still, as first one and then another turned up a side alley or knocked at a door and disappeared within. Fearing to be recognised, Anna kept her eyes upon the ground. For in house after house that she passed— white houses with green shutters and lace curtains, houses standing back from the road in large gardens, houses like Norman châlets—she knew the daughters of the retired business men or sea-captains who owned them. They were the richest men on the island, owners or captains of deep-sea boats, coasters, trawlers, or tunny-boats. Anna saw their daughters leaning from their windows or guessed they were in their bedrooms. With their fine clothes and head-dresses, they were the fairy princesses of her childhood's dreams—lovely ladies who gazed across the sea while they busied themselves with delicate needlework.

Anna did not pass unnoticed : more than one of these girls had recognised the diadem-like head-dress of Arzon and Monks' Island ; yet none called out her name in greeting. She reached the oldest part of the town and came to the long garden wall of the Presbytery. Facing it was the big inn which summer-time would find so crowded. Anna hurried down the straight slope towards the church in the distance. She passed four or five farms with their huddled outbuildings on her right. Before her were little orchards reaching to the shore, whose walls at high tide were washed by the waves.

Anna stopped short with beating heart. For there at the foot of the hill the rough winding road passed close to the long slate roof of her home, set at right angles to the road, whose shadow on summer mornings fell upon the sea. She strained both ears and eyes, but there was neither sound nor stir. Before the house was a patch of sloping land with an orchard of gnarled and stunted apple-trees beyond. Within a few feet of a hedge of gooseberry bushes were the mussel-beds which the tides now covered and now left bare. Everything seemed as impoverished and as neglected as ever, though she had noticed it less at that time.

Anna made her way to the familiar door. She went in and found her father sitting in the dark low-pitched room. He was mending a net with one end hooked over a nail in the wall.

' Anna ! You here ? '

He threw down his wooden needle : allowing the net to fall, he went to kiss his daughter.

' They've sent you home then ? '

' Oh no, father.'

' They keep you well tied to Penmur, I must say ! I had to take quite a trip to see you. And then you come home like this without a word of warning ! Have you taken pity upon your old father at last, and come back to look after him ? I hope you have ! '

He drew back the better to see her. A sense of great joy possessed him. His eyes glowed ; he stretched out his hands. Once more he said :

' You have, Anna, haven't you ? '

Anna put her white bundle upon her father's chair :

' You can see very well that I haven't got my grey box. There's all I've brought with me. But here's some fine pippins that they've sent from Penmur.' She finished more tenderly : ' You know it's not possible to do what you want—least of all, just now.'

' Then why have you come ? '

' What if I've come to consult you ? '

Corentin began to laugh loudly. ' That's a good one ! Consult me ? '

' Not on my own account. It's for my uncle and aunt. But it'll take a long time to explain. We can talk it over better to-night.'

' Are you staying the night ? '

' If you don't mind.'

' Please yourself ! Your brother's bed is still there. Consult me ? You ought to know by this time that I don't trust your uncle or aunt if they ask me to do anything. If they're out to make me look a fool, you can hold your tongue, and they can keep their apples. I'll have nothing to do with it.'

Anna knew that she must answer him. Choosing her words, she said :

' I shouldn't be here if they weren't serious.'

At once his face cleared, as he said : ' All right, then ! Take off your apron—it's much too good to work in.'

Pointing to the fire-place at the end of the room, he went on :

' I'll get eggs and potatoes and coffee. There's a ham smoking up there—you remember, don't you ? You can cut yourself a couple of slices. We'll take a walk when we've had it. There's plenty of folks who'll be glad to see you again.'

Turning at the door, he said as he went out : ' If the daily woman asks for me, tell her I'm in the garden ; say that this morning she's to look after the cows, as there's somebody else to do the cooking.'

The girl was left alone in the room which had belonged to her mother, in her time the most beautiful and one of the most shiftless women upon the island. A crucifix hung over the bed of rich figured walnut which still stood on the right of the fire-place :

' That's good ! The crucifix is still here for me to pray before,' Anna thought. The gilt chimney-clock and the old chest in which the children's spare clothes had been kept had both disappeared, sold to pay her father's debts.

Anna crossed the living-room and went into her brothers' room, where she was to sleep that night. Except for a bed, a chair, a dozen or so empty bottles, and a small cask with a mug under the tap, the room was bare.

She went back to the hearth, where she raked the cinders together, laid on the grass and dry twigs and lit them. As the flames darted up, the door was flung open.

' Somebody here ? Oh ! You're Miss Anna, are you ? '

Anna turned to see an old woman she had known in the town years before. ' You've come to get my father's dinner, have you ? ' she said.

' Yes, I do every day when he's not fishing.'

' Well, you needn't do it to-day, because I'm here. My father said you'd better look after the cows. How many are there ? '

' Only two now, I'm sorry to say ! There used to be four.'

' You take them to the meadow, I suppose ? '

' Yes, that's right.'

Working her toothless gums and peering suspiciously at the girl, who merely turned her head as she bent over the fire, the old woman cried shrilly :

' I suppose you've come back to look after him ? '

Anna's young laughter echoed through the bare farm-house, a reminder of old times :

' Oh no ! you needn't fear that. Come to-morrow as usual ; I shan't be here.'

The old woman went away.

' She's quite old,' thought Anna. ' Why did he pretend that it was a young girl who came to do his housework ? . . . Ah yes ! it was just another dodge of his to get me back from Penmur.'

She was sad although she felt relieved. In a short time the omelette was ready, the slices of ham were cooked and the pot of water hung before the fire.

' Well, my girl,' her father said as he came in, ' that omelette smells good.'

He had picked some salad and brought in a supply of potatoes. Then he went straight to the boys' room, where he stayed for almost a quarter of an hour. Anna was not anxious : she was accustomed to her father's ways. She laid the cloth on the rickety table, and was about to call her father when he came towards her from the next room saying : ' Well, Anna ; how do you think I'm looking ? Not bad for an old 'un, am I ?

I'm only joking, Anna ; though I have smartened myself
up a bit in honour of the occasion.'

He had combed his hair and his beard. Instead of his
working clothes he now wore a brown tweed suit that
gave him the air of a retired army officer. His bronzed
face and his tall, spare and upright figure both suggested
this. His eyes in particular, with their sparkle and their
cunning, hinted at the adventurous man that he was and
at the brave and resolute man that he might have been.
Already his breath smelt of aniseed. '

' Yes, you look too young and handsome,' Anna said.
' You'll make me look quite shabby when we call on your
friends. I haven't brought my best head-dress or my
apron that I wear at festivals.'

After a moment's pause she went on : ' I've no heart
for finery.'

Corentin was pleased at her praise. He drew up one
of the big chairs to the table and began to eat. Anna
busily served her father and herself scarcely sat down.

It was a cheerful meal. Corentin told the girl how he
spent his days, speaking with such animation that he
might well have been one of that island stock and a
fisherman all his life. In spirit he belonged to the
minstrels who wandered through Brittany in the Middle
Ages; to the bards called in at wedding feasts; to the old
sailors who yarn to the rest of the crew after their meal
on days when a calm sea and a fair wind leaves them
free to idle. Like theirs his eyes were full of restless
dreams ; like them he was often drunk ; like them in his
cups he forgot alike his age and his miserable life.

Anna, wise with the wisdom of the two different
streams flowing through her veins, listened to him with
a tender pity. While she laughed with him at times, she

asked herself how such a man could be expected to judge between her uncle and aunt, not realising that the goodness of his heart still remained practically unimpaired.

' Yes, Anna, le Morbihan and the sea have got into my blood. The sea's a curse to a landsman like I was when I married your mother. She was born by it ; was always unhappy away from it and half mad with joy when she got back to it. The sea begrudged me my farmer's life. First it took my living from me, then both my sons. Still I bear it no ill-will. It may be a poor trade, but it's full of life. If my brother wanted me to come back to Penmur to work and share the profits of the farm, I should send him about his business.'

' He's no longer well off.'

' So he says. That's an old yarn. But in the linen cupboard or behind the beer-barrel or a beam, there must be a good old stocking.'

' Father,' Anna said as she poured him out a tumbler full of cider, ' you've been reading the serial stories in the newspapers.'

' Not very often.'

' Oh, yes, you have.'

' I do of an evening. I'm so lonely here. I'm glad you'll be here to-night, my girl.'

' But I'm going in the morning.'

' Ah well ! we'll make the best of to-day then. I'll take you round to see the captains I know. You'll meet some of their smart daughters : they're quite as smart as church statues and a good deal livelier, I can tell you. When I pass their windows and hear them laughing, I think to myself, No girls like that round Penmur.'

' You're quite wrong : before the war we were gay enough.'

' I know all about the war. There are no young captains left round here. They are all out mine-sweeping or chasing the submarines. Let's have a drop to drink their health in ! '

' You've had enough for now. And this afternoon you'll have more when we're out calling.'

' A little fresh air will soon cure that. So let's hear no more about it. And fill up my glass. It smells of aniseed—like the strings of a mandolin when a Spaniard has just touched them. Look ! I'll stand up, and you can see if I am steady on my feet or not. Do I look as though I ought to stay at home ? '

She looked at him, alert, handsome, and devil-may-care. More anxiously than on her arrival she asked herself : ' What will he say when I tell him about Gildas this evening ? What was the use of sending me here ? '

They spent the afternoon paying visits to friends on the island. Many of these were the retired captains, whose houses were furnished to the taste of their fairy-tale daughters of Anna's imagining. Others, less prosperous, were old naval men who proudly displayed their shell-work boxes from India or Oceania, or a picture in black and white of a frigate in full sail upon a blue sea, with some such inscription as ' The *Juno*, lost in 1869 in the South Seas.'

One of their visits was to an old nurse who had brought up four ' young ladies ' on the mainland. This Mlle Yvonne gave her unexpected visitors warm welcome. She chatted of Anna's mother in the days of her youthful beauty : in Anna's honour she opened a bottle of comfits that had been hidden away since a long-past christening ; she led Anna herself into the trim garden held in common by the tenants of the block of four houses. Here from a south wall she picked the finest and most golden mimosa sprays that she could find. As once she had decked her young mistresses, so now she tucked one sprig in Anna's hair, another in the front of her dress, and gave her a spray to carry. Stepping back to look at her, she said : ' No one could wish to set eyes on a more beautiful bride than you, Anna Maguern. When your wedding comes off, you must invite me to it. Yours will be the last wedding gown I shall see, before I go to Paradise.'

She expected to see a radiant smile, but none came. Though Anna looked gratefully at her, Yvonne saw that her glance was less for herself than Corentin, as he bent over a plant near the water-butt. Kissing Anna, she said :

' Keep your secrets, my dear. I won't intrude on them any more.'

Soon afterwards father and daughter took their leave. They continued their way among the scattered houses with their walled or hedged gardens that dotted both slopes of the island. It was late before they made their last call and turned homeward along the path that wandered across the low promontory. On each side of the poor pastures and moorland the sea surged past with the glow of the setting sun on it, swirling on to the channel of Locmariaquer. The currents were swift and dangerous, especially between the islands of Jument, Gavr'innis, and Berder. Berder was beautiful with pines : green and glowing against the sky, they were reflected clear and sparkling in the water. Though the wind filled both its sails, a big black-hulled boat made little way towards Arradon and the River Vannes ; two small sloops, however, running with the tide, sailed so effort-lessly that their crews dozed on the foredeck.

Near a hamlet whose inn he knew well Corentin stopped short. Climbing a high bank, he pointed to the curve of the coast.

' If I weren't so tired, I'd go down to fish. It seems to me the wind's getting up, and there'd be a good catch to-morrow. What's the matter with you, Anna ? Can't you wait a minute ? But still I suppose you want to tell me about this affair of Jean-Guillaume's and your Aunt Marie's.'

A drunkard's laughter echoed down the lonely road. Then Corentin began to feel weak, and took his daughter's arm, saying :

' All right, we'll get along, if that's what you're worry-ing about. You shall tell me all about it before I go to bed. At my time of life a man doesn't need to work to get sleepy. . . . I'm not hungry.'

Anna reproached or encouraged her father as she helped him along. He staggered from the effects of the wine, cider, and coffee which he had drunk. She was ashamed, and when in the growing darkness they went by the village houses to reach the farm, she pretended not to see the neighbours who waved to her.

When they arrived, the wind had risen as Corentin had predicted. Anna lit the fire, while her father sat on the edge of the bed, holding out his hands to warm them. He watched her as she went to and fro. A single idea possessed his mind, though the state of semi-idiocy to which drink and physical weariness had brought him deprived him of power to express it. Anna could see how his eyes rolled and his mouth twitched, as he tried to attract the attention which she would not give him. Surely she was not to be questioned at a time like this ? To expect advice from a man in such a state was sheer folly. Yet she knew that there would be no escape. As she went into the room where she was to sleep that night, she heard her father's voice :

' Anna ? '

' What is it ? '

' Are you bent on keeping me awake ? Before the evening's out I want to know why Jean-Guillaume and Marie have sent you. Let's have it now, d'you hear ? You'd better, if you don't want me to raise the roof.'

He began to shout so violently that the neighbours might well have thought him the victim of some attack. In her early childhood Anna had seen her mother's method of mastering Corentin, who thrashed her often. In her turn the girl stood frowning at him from the middle of the room, and, enunciating every syllable that his fuddled mind might grasp her words, said resolutely :

' If you don't stop shouting at once, I shall go.'

More quietly he answered her : ' I'm not stopping you, but before you go you may as well say what you came for.'

' I will, if you'll undress and get into bed.'

' All right, Anna dear ! Promise you'll tell me. Though you may not think so, I've still got my wits about me.'

' I'll be back in five minutes.'

When she returned, she went to his bed and leaned over the wooden rail at the foot. With great compassion she gazed on the wasted man her father had become. Now somewhat cowed, he looked back at her.

He was lying on his back, his hands under the dirty sheet and the quilt which rats had gnawed in places. His protruding cheek-bones and skeleton-like forehead and nose were still more pronounced in the light of the glimmering lamp set on the chimney-piece. His eyes were merely two black cavities and his pointed chin threw a dark shadow over his shrivelled neck.

The night was stormy, and through the cracked walls draughts of wind blew gustily, making the lamp flicker. Light and shadow moved across the man's unstirring head. His impassivity beneath these changes gave him something of the appearance of a dead man. Yet Anna felt that beneath their lids his eyes were watching her. Slowly she said :

' Cousin Gildas at the front has written to say he wants to be a priest.'

Corentin raised his head and Anna saw his eyes flash.

' He must be mad.'

' Well, that's what his father thinks. But Aunt Marie doesn't.'

' Well, what do you think about it, my girl ? '

His head fell back wearily upon the pillow. Yet his eyes, Anna saw, continued to sparkle in the dim light of the lamp.

' I don't know what to think,' Anna answered. ' He's coming on leave very soon.'

' When ? '

' Any time now.'

' Show him you're fond of him, and he'll soon forget his wonderful idea.'

' It's his place to show he's fond of me. Still, he has a little.'

' Let him go on doing it, then.'

' What, now that he's begun Latin lessons ? '

' That's all right. You'll be able to sing the *Oremus* together. Just like a girl to put obstacles in the way ! You're not going to let a chance like this pass, are you ? It's a good farm and Gildas is a fine young chap, and what's more he's the eldest son now. . . .'

As though the news had given him strength Corentin stretched out his arms towards his daughter. Although his eyes were still bleared, he no longer spoke like a drunken man. He said entreatingly :

' You don't say anything, but I know you've a good heart. You'd like to marry your cousin for your own sake, wouldn't you, Anna ? But in any case you'll marry him to help your poor old father, won't you now ? If you're a servant, you can't help me much. But if you're a farmer's wife, it'll be easy enough.'

He was tired with the effort which he had made to speak. His eyes closed, and though his lips moved no sound came from them.

Anna went quietly from the room, leaving the door ajar that she might hear her father, should he call for help when his drunken fit reached its worst. The wind came howling from the sea in squalls that grew steadily in strength. Above the plank ceiling the roof groaned and shook. Gusts that stormed into the loft with the noise of pistol shots came between the loose slates. Shrill whistling noises were followed by the thud of heavy slabs of the stone roof as the wind lifted them and let them fall.

After a sleepless hour her father called to Anna three times. At the third time she said :

' Go to sleep now ! You can tell me in the morning ! '

' No I can't. It's the islands ! They're all shouting—
can't you hear them ? '

' You're talking nonsense, father. Islands can't
shout ! '

' It's plain you don't belong here any more. I can
hear them shouting their names one after another :
" Hoedic ! Hoedic ! Houat ! Houat . . ." It's enough
to drive you mad.'

In the silence which followed Anna thought of Gildas'
leave and of what she must do then. Pulling the sheet
over her face to keep off the whistling gusts which blew
in from the sea, she found herself thinking :

' It won't be Jean-Guillaume or anybody else
that decides what he'll do. It'll be me. His soul has
been put in my keeping, and I'm not nearly strong
enough to decide. Although he's coming back to see
the family and the farm, he's coming to see me too and
to find out what I think about this idea of his. He'll
know as soon as he looks at me : for I'm not one of those
girls who laugh to order. My face will give me away.
I'm no different from most girls of my age. Even before
I came to Penmur and knew Gildas, I always wanted to
be married and to have children. And now I've got to
say either : " Never mind me—make your own plans "
or else, " Don't give me up, Gildas ; you can't now—
we're too fond of each other. . . ." I thought father
would answer like that. Ah, I wish I hadn't heard what
he said. Then God might have given me the idea of
saving his soul. A more self-sacrificing girl would want
to do that. Although the world wouldn't know it, she'd
get another to heaven. People do things like that. I've
heard so in sermons and read it in books. Sacrifice
brings its own reward. A friend or relative or even a

stranger makes surrender of some personal joy to the Master of all joy, and then a man like my father is put upon the right road again and given strength beyond his desert. But I can't do it. My soul's too poor to make others rich, even my father's. That's certain, and I can't throw away my own happiness for his. Time enough to think of all that when I've been cast off, and I've to make up my mind to live without him whether at Penmur or anywhere else. What I shall do then, I can't think. I wish I were small again, and hadn't to suffer like this.'

It was her communion with the saints that gave this unlettered Breton her knowledge of our finite world. She sighed as she murmured her thoughts aloud.

' Are you crying, Anna ? '

' Go to sleep, father.'

' How can you expect anybody to sleep with a gale like this ? I've been lying here listening to it. Hark, the wind's crying, too ! All the while you can hear the moaning of Baguenhir Reef. You know where it is, don't you ? The one past the Buissons de Méaban.'

' I can't hear anything.'

' The wind won't stay in that quarter. You'll see by the next tide. It'll be in the west to-morrow, with a fine day. And a good thing too ! It's no use thinking of geese, but there'll be duck there still. I'll take my gun out in the morning. It seems a long night even with you here. You can guess what it's like when I'm alone.'

Once more he was silent. Anna went back to the thought of her threatened love. Her human heart and her eternal soul waged their fight within her, and neither had the victory.

When she got up early in the morning, she found her father in a heavy sleep. On a sheet of paper she scrawled :

' You had such a bad night, I didn't want to wake you. I'm off to the harbour. I expect I shall find a small boat to take me to Arradon or somewhere near, so that I can get to Vannes. I'm going to see Gildas' godmother, before I go back to Penmur. She keeps the grocer's shop near S. Vincent harbour. She will put me up for the night, and early to-morrow morning I shall go back to the farm. Your affectionate Anna.'

She added the note to the pocket-knife, purse and tinder-box lying on her father's chair. Noiselessly closing the door, she hurried across the yard and took the road to the village. Her father was right. The gale of the night before had dwindled to a gentle but cold westerly wind. A mist was in the air, but there was a glow behind the mist that suggested a warm day to come. Anna walked quickly, her one care preoccupying her mind and leaving her sad and uncertain. In earlier days she might well have been the lady-in-waiting of some duchess of Brittany ; for she was graceful of carriage and proud of bearing.

Towards evening the wind changed and blew steadily from the south, driving the mists before it. On the south-east side of the island Corentin followed the Brouel road. Limping a little, in an old cloak that hung to his knees and with a soft felt hat thrust forward over his face, he kept his eyes on the ground in front of him, either that none should recognise him, or because the too familiar road had lost all interest. Before he left the higher road behind him, he looked to see if the lighthouse-keepers had been punctual in lighting their lamps. In

front of him he saw the fixed light at Port Navalo ;
while out at sea, like windmills with arms of light,
sweeping the sky with their great rays, Teignouse
flashed redly at five-second intervals and Goulphar on
Belle Île threw its double white beam every ten seconds.
Since neither Four Light nor Grands Cardinaux were
to be seen, he concluded that the night was mistier than
he had thought.

Dropping his head again, he trudged on to the hamlet
of Brouel which, like Guerno, had a wretched inn.   He
rarely passed this by, but always stopped, on the pretext of eating or warming himself.   Because the night
threatened to be cold, he drank two glasses of home-
brew, and at once went down to the beach.   Now he
could openly carry the gun which he had kept hidden
beneath his brown cloak.   This gun was a big-bore Le-
faucheux, in excellent state except for a crack near the
end of the barrel. Smoke escaped each time Corentin fired.

As the sun was setting, he hid behind the hedge of a
poor meadow on the far side of which were the mussel-
beds. The swift currents of the estuary as they ran down
to the channels were still streaked gold and blue by the
dying sun. The sound of a shot prepared Corentin for
the flock of wild duck which with whirring wings came
flying over the island. He waited until they had left
the water before he let loose his charge of number
nought. He brought down two, which fell into the next
field.   The first flock was followed by a second, the
second by a third, fourth, and fifth.   The shots which
rang out from various parts of the island were a sign
that many poachers were abroad.

Half an hour after sunset Corentin left the shelter of
his hedge. He knew that there would be no more duck

until daybreak, when they would make for the bays
of Rhuys and Quiberon. Groping through the dark
fields, he came at last upon the fallen birds. He
stumbled over a ridge of turf and clutched with both
hands at the earth in an attempt to regain his feet. His
weariness was stronger than his will. His eyes closed.
With pain in all his limbs he lay stretched full length
upon the ground, as helpless as on the days when his
drunkenness was worst. He made vain attempts to call
for aid. The stiffened muscles of his arms slowly relaxed.
His head rolled into a hollow at a level lower than his
feet. He lost consciousness.

For an hour he did not move. A sudden sense of
danger awakened him ; he contrived first to sit up and
then to struggle to his feet. He felt for his gun in a
furrow near by and picked it up. Obeying his hunter's
instinct he fumbled next for the pair of duck which he
had been carrying before his fall. He found them, tied
them by the feet, and slung them from his neck.

With painful effort he made his way from the field.
Finding his gun heavy upon his shoulder, he took it and,
using it as a stick, succeeded in reaching the road. He
stumbled on and was almost at the end of his strength
when he reached the first houses in the village. Failing
to take his customary turning, he found himself in the
road by the church which led to his farm, but several
hundred yards away from it. At first he did not realise
this. When he understood the mistake which he had
made, and knew that yet another effort was required of
him, he gave a low howl like a beast in agony.

Either no one heard him or no one understood how
desperate was his appeal. Probably any fisherman or
villager who heard his cry thought it one of the usual

night noises, or one of those jokes in which holiday-makers, who come from as far away as Paris, find delight.

Corentin staggered along clinging to the wall on his right, and so keeping his balance when dizziness threatened. His one thought was now of walking straight. With each new step his strength ebbed slowly from him ; his sight began to fail. His head was so swollen with blood that twice he had to take off his hat and stand still to allow the cold air to relieve the pressure. His brain became empty of all thought : still he staggered on.

The wall seemed longer than most. He decided that it must be the wall of the presbytery garden. He came at last to the doorway. Muttering to himself : ' I'm about done,' he rang. Behind the door he heard a muttered conversation :

' Go to the door, Marie. There's a ring.'

' Yes, I thought so too, father. But can it be, as late as this ? It's nine o'clock.'

' Don't worry about the time. It may be someone who is sick. I'm here if I'm wanted.'

It was indeed a sick man whom Marie found sprawling across the threshold with his gun by his side and his brace of duck about his neck. When he spoke, she heard only half his words and had to guess the rest :

' I'm Corentin Maguern. I want the priest to give me the Sacraments. I'm done.'

Half an hour later Corentin, whom an obliging neighbour had wheeled back to his own farm in a barrow, was lying in his bed half-unconscious. The large bare room was but feebly lit by the oil lamp. The priest had gone, having administered the Sacraments, which the sick man received half-consciously, raising himself several times and managing at last to jerk out :

'Go and find Anna . . . at Vannes . . . grocer's shop . . . her relative keeps it . . . near Port S. Vincent.'

It was not easy at so late an hour to find a man willing to cross the Gulf to go up the Vannes River.

The young woman from the next farm suggested a plan :

'I know,' she exclaimed. 'I'll take my little boy along with me, and then I'll not be afraid.'

The woman had remembered that before Anna had left the island a certain young sailor had shown himself so greatly attracted by her beauty and housewifely skill that there had been much talk of a marriage between the two.

It was to the old squat house of this Matthieu Hervouët —hutch rather than house, whose tarred roof covered only two rooms, bedroom above and kitchen below—that the farmer's wife led her small son, drowsily proud to walk the dark roads by night. He shook off his drowsiness when on the harbour side of the village they came in sight of the fishing boats rolling at anchor beyond the rocks. His pride became pleasure when he was allowed to throw a pebble on to the roof of Hervouët's house. Soon the window was thrown up, and the head and shoulders of a big fair man in shirt-sleeves appeared. In no good-humoured voice he called out :

'What's the matter ? What are you up to, Marie, throwing stones on a man's roof at this time of night to wake him up ? '

'Sorry, Matthieu, but it's serious. Old Maguern's very ill—not expected to live. Someone's got to go to Vannes at once.'

'Well, I'm not going. You'll have to try somebody else.'

As he began to close the window, she shouted :

' Whoever goes has to call for Anna Maguern at the grocer's, and bring her back here early to-morrow.'

After a short silence the man said : ' All right, I'll go.' The farmer's wife smiled in the darkness. As she took her boy's hand and turned to go, she heard the voice of Matthieu again : ' The wind's in the right quarter. I'll go, Marie.' He added something that sounded like ' Thank you.' She smiled again.

Before sunrise, when the sky was just beginning to glimmer over the still dark sea, the first fishing boats passed Arz Island and, heading inward, reached the River Vannes. Towards them, with little wind to catch its one large sail, a single green-hulled smack was tacking. The *Espérance* was quickly recognised, and there was much speculation as to what Matthieu Hervouët was doing on the river at that early hour.

When the smack passed through the fleet of lighters, barges, sloops, and Bourgneuf cat-boats, a pretty girl was seen holding the tiller, while a young man swung the boom. Although they did not recognise her, since she wore the diadem-like head-dress of Monks' Island, those aboard the fleet gave her the silent salute which they would have given a procession on a feast day. She neither spoke nor smiled, but merely nodded her thanks. They guessed her grief.

The little fleet had become separate sails scattered over the Gulf ; the windows in the village of Arz were sparkling in the sun, and the currents bore the rippling water and drifting seaweed before them, as Anna opened the farm-house door.

Her father was lying on his bed with his eyes closed and his face red and swollen. Although he seemed asleep, he moaned and tried to speak, but Anna could not distinguish his words. Several times she bent her smooth face near his head buried in the deep pillow, saying: 'I'm here, father. Try to speak. I won't leave you any more.'

He made no sign, although his eyes stirred slightly beneath the stretched red lids.

On the hearth, where embers from the fire of the night before still glowed, stood an earthenware pot full of lime water covered with a slate. The woman called in the night before had forced the sick man to take several spoonfuls of this remedy. He had spat these from him in disgust.

The woman was still in the house, wandering aimlessly from room to room. She had slept in Anna's bed. In a leisurely manner she tidied her dishevelled hair so that Anna might realise she was waiting for her wages. As Anna gave her the money, she said:

'It's my belief your father won't last the day. He's not the first on the island I've seen taken with a syncope, they call it. There doesn't seem to be anything you can do for them. They can't eat and they last no time at all. The great thing is not to give them liquor, however much they ask for it.'

'You can leave all that to me.'

'But I shouldn't mind a drop myself just to pick me up.'

'You're welcome.'

'But you mustn't give him any. I'll be back again to-night to sit up with you, Miss Anna.'

Until about three o'clock in the afternoon Corentin

remained in a state of coma. As the level rays of the late sun, streaming through the small window, fell upon her father's face, Anna saw that his eyes were open. She went to his bed. In the effort to recognise his daughter his face was convulsed and his eyes were sunk deeper than ever. Anna bent over him. With strange intentness he stared at her, and managed to utter these five words in a loud voice: 'Don't set yourself against God.'

He went unanswered. For Anna's emotion had temporarily mastered her, and she could find no word to say. As she bent over him once more, she saw that his eyes were again rolling under their lids. Only the sick man's groaning broke the stillness of the room.

He grew weaker as the hours passed. The doctor had been summoned by telegram, but before he arrived that night Corentin was dead.

Two days later his body was carried to the church, followed by a few friends from the island. Jean-Guillaume had come alone from Muzillac. He had debated at length before he came; for the old feud still rankled with him. That morning when he reached Corentin's house, he stayed in the yard; for, guessing how pitifully poverty-stricken he would find everything, he could not bring himself to enter. He talked with the few sailors, poachers, and other companions of Corentin who had come at the tolling of the bell. On the pretext of settling an account with the notary at Vannes, he left immediately the service was over. Because of his love for her, before he went he called Anna to him. In her borrowed mourning shawl she came out of the empty house. He said to her:

'Now you've lost your father, you can always have a

home with us. Clear up here, and then come back to Penmur.'

As he turned to go, he saw that she was weeping. The black cloth that she had put over the fine white lace of her diadem added to her sorrowful beauty. He would have been amazed had he known what she was thinking :

' He's right enough when he says that I've lost father. But if he'd come inside he'd have known that I've lost Gildas too. He'll know and so will Aunt Marie when I get back again.'

CHAPTER XI

PLANS

FOUR days later Anna came within sight of the Penmur fields and the moor with its trees bowed by the wind. With Corentin buried under the great elms of the island churchyard and the two boys away on the high seas, the last of the Maguerns had left the sea-washed farm which had given them so poor a livelihood. From a slope she saw the roof with its tufts of house-leek, and thought to herself : ' I've nobody of my own left, so I'll always have to live with other people now.'

Her belongings made a bulkier package than on the day when she had left for Monks' Island. Pausing by the thickets of gorse and the stunted trees at the end of the moor, she untied her bundle, and taking from it two sheets she spread them on the low bushes. She continued her way to the farm by the path through the wind-swept coppice. Denise, carrying her baby, gave her a warmer welcome than usual. After the two women had exchanged a long kiss, Anna said humbly :

' You remember the last time my father was here, Denise, and Aunt Marie put those sheets out upon the moor . . . ? '

With a nod of her head she indicated the thicket :

' You go and fetch them in—they've certainly had time to dry.'

154

Anna crossed the farm-yard. Her aunt and her cousins gathered round her, the children shouting for joy at her return ; for they were not yet old enough to understand grief.

Jean-Guillaume heard their cries and came to join them. Leading his wife and the girl into the empty room where the boys slept, he said

' Well, did your father have anything to say before he died ? '

He was taking a load of quick-lime to a nearby field, and had brought his goad into the room with him. He had it clenched in his right fist, and now raised it like a lance above his shoulder. Resentment against his brother and anger against Gildas showed in his eyes. Marie Maguern, her hands clasped in her lap, waited for the words which she thought were to bring her grief. Nevertheless, she was determined to uphold her son. Anna knew that she was about to give judgement upon herself, yet she was as resolute as they ; for she was of the same stock. She answered Jean-Guillaume :

' I asked him about Gildas.'

' What did he say—did he decide with me or against me ? '

' Against you. He said : " Don't set yourself against God." '

It was the mother who first broke the silence which followed. In her clear voice she said :

' I knew he would. He was a sinner like the rest of us, but he was a Christian at heart.'

Jean-Guillaume clenched the handle of the goad more tightly. He said : ' It was your idea, Marie, to ask my brother. I agreed for the sake of peace, but I've never paid any attention to his opinion and I'm not going to now. I stick to what I've said before.'

His wife unclasped her hands and fumbled in her pocket.

' Just a minute ! Here's a letter from Gildas.'

' When did that come ? '

' The postman brought it when you were loading the quick-lime.'

She unfolded the letter. She had no need to read it ; for already she knew its contents :

' He'll be here on leave to-morrow morning. He's coming on the fast train to Questembert.'

' Which ? '

' The half-past eight, of course.'

' Let Ange go to meet him.'

' Aren't you going then ? Surely you will ! If only I could drive now ! '

Her husband lowered the goad :

' I tell you Ange is to meet him. I shall go my own way ; I don't care what Corentin said.'

The two women heard his heavy tread through the living-room, where the children made way for him. He shouted to the oxen as they started, and again as the team turned to the left at the bottom of the yard. Marie Maguern looked at Anna, who had not stirred.

When Gildas returned on the following day, he would find a divided household : his father antagonistic and Anna doubly unhappy. Now that only her aunt saw her the girl did not conceal her anguish, though she kept back her tears. The older woman, who had seen much grief, reflected : ' She's got some courage.'

Then Anna came close to her and said :

' I've got lots of sewing to do for my mourning. . . .

' Yes, of course.'

' If you'll let me, I'll go to our dressmaker at Muzillac in the morning. I'll work with her and come back at night.'

The mother drew her close. Hugging her she whispered that the children might not hear :

' I think that's a good plan of yours.'

She still held Gildas' letter. Glancing at it again, she added :

' He won't be spending much time with us—he says that he'll be going in the evening.'

' So soon ? Why ? '

' If I must tell you, my dear, I think it's because of you. But you can still go to Muzillac ; for you don't want to see him, do you ? '

' The last thing I wish is for him to see me again.'

Her aunt was at first astonished by the answer. Then she understood, and giving the girl another long friendly look, she said :

' You're a true Christian.'

Each went her way to the morning's work.

CHAPTER XII

RENUNCIATION

GILDAS was weary when he reached Penmur on this first leave since the beginning of his service. Other men from these parts had been home several times : they told stories of the trenches rather than of the fighting ; they drank with their friends in the inns, proud of the attention paid to even their trivial remarks, and everywhere, accompanied by friends and relatives, were to be seen out walking. But Gildas had not been home.

The captain had said to him one day : ' You haven't asked for leave, Maguern.' ' Not yet, sir.' This answer made the officer look curiously at the young Breton, who saluted him. He thought : ' Perhaps he has no relatives and nothing to go back to. It's a pity ; for I'd be glad to give leave to such a good fellow.'

On this occasion, however, Gildas had asked for it. His train was crowded with other men going on leave. At odd intervals he had dozed, his head upon a neighbour's shoulder ; had walked across Paris from the Gare de l'Est to the Gare d'Orléans ; had slept again in the second train, and then at daybreak, with no word to anyone, not even his own countrymen, he had stared lovingly at the passing country-side. For they were nearing Brittany. With every mile evidences of his much-loved province grew plainer. The slopes were

covered with furze and bramble. There were stretches
of moor with their low walls ; a sleepy white horse ;
whiffs of iodine from seaweed ; long vistas of magnificent beeches ; black and white cattle ; apple orchard
after apple orchard ; while above, the scurrying clouds
were driven before the wind. Granite was everywhere :
about the windows, doors, and copings of houses ; as
boundaries to the fields—Breton granite with its faint
sparkle of mica showing through the lichen.

As Gildas gazed, his weariness of the night before
disappeared. He saw a small town ahead. Here at last
was his own country. Ten minutes before the train
ran in he was ready at the window, and was the first of the
three Questembert men on the platform.

' Hullo, Ange ! How's mother and father and the
children and poor Denise ? '

' You're looking well. A bit thin, but a real soldier.'

' Well I am one ! But how's everybody ? '

' All very well.'

' You can't help being a bit anxious . . . when you
come back . . .'

He broke off for a moment and then went on :
' The mare's looking all right, anyway. Mind the
corner.'

It was an unnecessary remark. For Ange was a good
driver, and the trap bowled along steadily. There was a
soft breeze. White clouds were scattered over the blue
sky ; men and women, houses and trees looked the more
joyous for the streaming sunlight. In the streets of
Questembert, Gildas looked eagerly among the passers-by
to find a friend and give him greeting. For his heart was
crying out : ' I'm back from the war ; it's good to be
back ! It's good to be home ! ' But in all the town

there was not one to greet the two boys sitting behind the fast-trotting mare.

At the end of an hour the trap turned from the Nantes-Vannes highroad into a lane on the left. Over the low hedge he could see the familiar moor again. He knew that in a moment more the sloping roof of his home would be in sight, with the smoke curling before the west wind. Though the mare was jolting them over the ruts, Gildas rose impulsively to his feet, and waved his cap so that anyone in the Penmur lanes and fields who saw and heard the rattle of the wheels over the pebbles should give news of his return to the rest.

A quarter of an hour earlier Anna had gone into Muzillac.

In a flat basket she carried a black dress and some odd pieces of stuff for repairing, and some linen to mend. She took the by-road to the town, as she wished to avoid meeting the trap. She might well have been a dressmaker going to her daily work. She looked straight before her, and saw neither fields nor fences nor thorny hedges. She knew the road so well that she reached and climbed each stile mechanically. At last she came to the lane between two houses, which ran into the high road opposite the smithy where the horses waited their turn. She opened a door to the left, and a bell tinkled. The dressmaker, who had been seated at her machine near the window, came forward shaking the threads from her apron.

' Good morning, Marie Dieudonnée. I've brought some work along.'

' Good morning, Anna ; how pale you are ! '

' It's just my heart. I've been walking too fast, and I

feel a little faint. . . . I've brought this old dress to make my mourning, and I want you to help me, if you don't mind.'

' Yes, I'll be only too glad. Has your aunt said that you can stop ? '

' Yes, she says I can stay all day.'

' They're good to you at Penmur, aren't they ? Sit down there by the geranium. Then you'll be able to see the people go by. Let me have your basket and your things. This is quite a surprise visit. But you'll be company for me, and I like that.'

' So do I.'

Anna again grew pale. The dressmaker pitied the girl whose heart was affected by so short a walk.

Ange and Gildas had drawn up in the farmyard. His mother was the first to greet the boy on leave. Her face was beaming as she ran towards him with out-stretched hands. She clasped him tight, and thought of the time when he would no longer be a soldier but a priest.

' Oh, Gildas, how I've longed for this ! '

They held each other, his grey-blue uniform pressed to her black clothes.

Alexis, Armandine, and Denise with the baby all waited their turn. When he had kissed them all, Gildas looked round the group and said :

' Where's father ? '

The children went back to their play. Jean-Guillaume, who had come home especially from Four Days Field, stood waiting by Denise's box-bed. He wore an old Sunday suit, much patched and mended, and his round felt hat, and was ready to return to his work. Gildas

went over to him, taking off his knapsack and standing
an empty bottle on the table. As his father made no
move, the boy hesitated and took off his cap.

' Well, come along,' the old man said.

He allowed Gildas to kiss him.

' I told you what I thought in my letter. As you
haven't answered, I suppose you are still of the same
mind.'

' Yes, father.'

' And so am I.'

There was grief as well as determination on their faces.
They stood there close together, the boy a little taller
than his father, and looked resolutely and sadly at each
other. But in the father's eyes was an anger that his
son's lacked.

' What gave you this idea of being a priest,
Gildas ? '

' I thought of it first when I was a small boy. I told
mother about it.'

' If you had only told me then, I shouldn't have stood
in your way. But it's too late now. What brought the
idea back ? '

' I expect it's because I've seen what the world's like,
lately.'

' Do you hope to help it, then ? '

' With God's grace.'

In the long silence which followed, Marie Maguern
wept quietly. The two men had more control. Looking
at his son's face as though he saw it for the first time,
Jean-Guillaume thought : ' He looks like an officer
already.' At the same time he remembered the day's
work which must be done, and said :

' You want to help the world. Yet you don't want to

help me, and I'm nearest to you. Soon Ange will have
to go, whether the war is over or not. He's nearly old
enough for his service. And even if you come through,
you'll be no more help to me.'

Gildas looked round at his youngest brother, Alexis,
who seemed sturdier than he remembered, but he had
not the courage to put his thought into words, and
merely pointed to him. How could he reproach his
father for this devotion to the farm ? Jean-Guillaume
straightened his shoulders as though he would shift a
burden. He said :

' I'm taking quick-lime to Four Days Field, Gildas.
It's badly needed down there, and I've brought along
a cartload to-day from the big heap which you'll
remember at Le Cormier.'

' Yes, father. What are you sowing in Four Days
Field ? '

Jean-Guillaume asked himself if it were not a hopeful
sign that the boy had put the question. He said :

' The year's getting on, and it's cold down there. I
shall sow spring oats. . . . I'll see you again at dinner,
but the work must be done. How long are you home
for ? '

Catching up her grandchild who was near Jean-
Guillaume, Marie Maguern said :

' I didn't have time to warn you that he's off again
to-night. He said so in his letter.'

' Off to-night ? Where ? '

At his harsh and angry gesture at Gildas, Denise
thought it best to leave. The three who remained might
have been judge, prisoner, and a mother who pleaded.
Jean-Guillaume stared first at his wife, and then more
resentfully at his son :

'Father'—Gildas did not flinch as he spoke—'I'm off to a school in the Vendée. They take grown-up men like me who want to be priests.'

'Will you learn Latin and that sort of thing?'

'Yes.'

'The war's not finished yet. And when it is, do you think they'll take you? You'll have nothing much beside your good looks. I suppose you think you'll be another little S. John with no clothes on your back and with no money for fees.'

His wife laid her hand on his arm:

'Now Jean-Guillaume! Don't let your anger run away with you. You won't let the boy want, when it comes to it, will you?'

'Oh, won't I, then? He doesn't care what happens to me, and I shan't give him a thing. Neither shall you, Marie, do you hear? And what's more, when he gets to the school, he can tell the director.'

'Yes, you can take my word as a Maguern,' Gildas said. 'It'll be the first thing I say after I get there.'

In spite of Marie Maguern's entreaty the old man remained sullen. In her anguish she now said to her boy:

'You won't part from your father like this, will you, Gildas? Stay for to-night at least. By the morning you'll both have forgotten your angry words.'

'I shan't,' Jean-Guillaume said.

His wife, very near to tears, turned to Gildas:

'Oh, son, son, do stay!'

He looked at her:

'No, I can't. The longer I stay, the harder it will be to go.'

Because she knew that he was right, she could find no

word to answer him. Jean-Guillaume pushed past the two. In silence they watched his burly figure silhouetted in the doorway, its long shadow reaching to their feet. A moment later he was gone to his work in Four Days Field.

'Come along, Gildas!' the mother said to her son. 'There's a lot I want to ask you. Letters don't say much.'

To have the privacy which was impossible in the house they went to the wind-swept orchard on the far side of the outbuildings. There beneath the few poor apple trees they walked and talked together. Despite her pleasure in this talk, Marie Maguern did not wholly forget the daily round of her household, and listened to the voices she heard on the other side of the wall. With her hands in her apron pockets she walked close by her son's side, glancing tenderly at him as she addressed him. Her joy increased as they talked; she realised that he had grown wiser and more resolute. He delighted her by his repetition of the words of comfort and of courage which he had heard so often from the chaplain of the 135th. He told her of the priest's devotion, his self-sacrifice, and his great understanding of the needs of men's souls and bodies alike. With pride he confided to her that the chaplain was now convinced of his own vocation, farmer's boy though he was.

Yet Marie Maguern was not without her fears. Possibly her son—possibly the chaplain—would be killed; man's resolution so often fails, and Gildas' probation would be a long one; above all, there was Jean-Guillaume's deep-rooted obstinacy.

Her mother's heart again found its strength in the trust which had so often sustained her. Her kind face smiled up at her son who, in order not to tire her, suited his step to hers.

That day the apple orchard was paradise for Marie Maguern. Often she looked at the blue sky through the branches, thanking God for the sweet interludes he grants to weary mothers.

' Let's talk a bit longer, Gildas. Denise is doing my work, so I shan't be behind when I go back.'

' Yes, Denise is a good worker.'

' Yes, sometimes she is.'

' Where's Anna ? I haven't seen her yet.'

His mother shivered, and for the first time dare not look into his face. Instinctively they stared before them : in their preoccupation neither saw the wide horizon ; while there was a new note in the woman's voice as she answered :

' She's the girl you should have married, Gildas, if you'd been free—but then you aren't now. Anna wanted to be out of the way to-day.'

' Why, is she grieving for her father ? '

' No, not that.'

There was a pause before he said :

' Well, it was best anyway.'

Marie Maguern glanced quickly at her son. The thought came to her also : ' He looks like an officer.'

It was near midday, and the sun was warm. His mother went indoors, but Gildas stayed in the farmyard telling his brothers, Armandine, and Denise about the war, and answering their questions about life in the trenches and in the devastated villages. They found it good to have him back, with his tanned face and affectionate smile. He told them story after story, as soldiers and travellers delight to do.

They all reproached him for leaving the farm so soon, but he gave no explanation. Each of them told him to look in his knapsack for a present, so that Gildas should know how much they cared for him. On the evening before the whole family had gone to the town to shop, or had searched Penmur for gifts to make to the soldier on his return to the front. And now in a few hours he would be gone again.

Their midday meal was almost silent. Except for Jean-Guillaume they had all talked freely during the morning. Their father was morose and bent on getting back to his work. His gloom spread to the rest : gradually their jokes and questions about the Front died into silence.

' Well, Gildas,' his father said, rising, ' you know where I'll be when you go. If you want to say good-bye, I'm in Four Days.'

Shortly afterwards, Ange harnessed the old mare and drove his brother to the presbytery of the next parish. Gildas paid a call on the aged rector, the confessor and friend of his boyhood days. The two men had a long and intimate talk.

Gildas had decided not to return to the district again until after his ordination. As he left the village, which lay in the wildest and most wooded part of the district, he grew disturbed at the thought of the coming talk with his father. Climbing to the highest point, he looked long and wistfully on every side. At length shaking the earth from his stick, he found the trap and was driven as far as the boundary between Grand Néant and Penmur. He left Ange, and by paths and cart-tracks reached his own more open country. On every side were the fields in which he had so often ploughed, manured, sown, and reaped. In the Somme trenches he had talked of Brittany with educated men, particularly with his friend the chaplain, and he now saw it with new eyes.

At a short distance from the field where his brother and Jean-Guillaume were working he stopped, sick at heart with the thoughts which crowded on him. He watched the two men plunge their shovels into the heaps of quick-lime and powdered earth with which the field was covered. With a circular movement they spread the manure and were half-hidden in a cloud of white dust.

Jean-Guillaume, who was the nearer to the hedge, did not hear Gildas jump the ditch nor see him cross the field. When he saw the soldier saluting him, he merely thrust his spade into the clods.

Wiping the lime from his face with his shirt-sleeve, the old man looked at his son. His weariness and the angry words which he had spoken that morning hardened his heart. Gildas longed for some sign of affection, but none came. Although Jean-Guillaume's wrath had died, the life which he led made him harsh. He held out his hand.

' Well, good-bye, my boy. If you're bent on this idea, it will be some time before I see you again.'

Gildas made no answer. He thought : ' Why doesn't such a good Christian as my father understand that I must obey this call of mine ? ' His father thought : ' Gildas has a good heart. How can he leave me in this fix ? '

Yet neither of them said what was in his heart. As they parted, Jean-Guillaume went on :

' The others have given you their presents. Well, that's all right. But I tell you again that I can't pay your fees. I can't.'

Gildas made a gesture as if to say, ' God will provide.'

He saluted his father. The old man scattered a spadeful of quick-lime, setting up a white cloud between them.

Gildas crossed the field and shook his brother's hand. At Penmur his mother's tenderness and the children's affection brought him a measure of comfort. It was getting dark when he left the farm.

At this moment Anna was leaving Muzillac with her basket of needlework. She heard the men in the fields as they finished their day's work. She had barely turned into the hilly road off the Vannes highway when the wind carried to her the sound of the rattling hooves of the chestnut in the distance. Hurriedly she found a gap in the hedge, climbed the slope and hid behind the broom bushes. Still clutching her basket, she stood very tense and pale. The trap went by with Alexis driving. Gildas, looking straight before him, smiled at the boy's jokes. He smiled out of kindness, yet his heart was heavy. Anna watched him with wistful eyes. For the last time, it might be, the lines of his face were etched upon her memory.

She was to treasure this picture in her heart. Now that he was gone she felt suddenly weary. For her the day was over : would she have the strength, she asked herself, to do this difficult thing of which she had been thinking during the day's work at the dressmaker's ?

She gave no heed to the passers-by. She no longer listened for the rattle of horses' hooves upon the road ; she walked more and more slowly. In her travail of spirit she cried aloud : ' O my people in heaven, help me ! '

Who can say that her cry went unheeded by the blessed saints above, and that at the throne of God prayers were not offered for her ? For the Maguerns,

it is not to be doubted, have added many saints to the
community of heaven. Among them in ancient times
were those husbandmen converted by S. Armel whom
the pagans had so oppressed, and who yet had been
patient under their oppression. There had been that
early Talbot, the first settler in the swamps and
forests where now Muzillac stood. This trapper and
forester had administered justice in those parts that
had no judge but he. Then there were the young virgins
in the twelfth century who had become nuns in Cornwall,
and taught its semi-barbarian daughters that purity
rejoices the heart of God and the heavenly host. Again,
there was Peter the ploughman, who with his wooden
ploughshare had tilled so much earth that he could
hardly sow half of it even with the help of his four sons.
There had been Blennoc who, though every beast in his
herd was swept away in a cattle plague, had not complained nor grown discouraged. There was Yvonnette,
the royalist, who by night had taken messages to the
faithful saying where their meeting-place should be, at
that time when only on the moors could they say Mass
or Vespers. And there were those many mothers who
uncomplainingly had spent themselves in endless toil.
Even Anna's mother by her repentance had joined that
saintly host. Who can say that the rest of the elect,
beholding the benediction poured out upon the earth,
did not cry ' Hosanna ! this day has a soul been blessed
because all her kinsmen have prayed for her ' ?

It may well be that they looked down upon the poor
girl who, basket on arm, had reached the boundary of
the moor. It had changed since that evening when Gildas
and Anna had crossed it together. As darkness drew on,
the wind died down. Anna searched for the spot where

they had talked. She stumbled upon it at length, recognising it by the gravel which neither heather nor gorse nor bracken had entirely hidden. Crossing herself, she knelt in the grass. She prayed : ' O God, willingly I give up love. I give up my youth ; my chance of marriage, my hope of children. I will bring up Denise's little one. But protect him and bring him back—not for me but for your service.' With a sorrowful smile this girl, steeped in the language of the Scriptures, added as she rose from her knees : ' You cannot refuse me this ; for it is your glory that I seek.'

Anna called upon the silent fields to be her witness that she accepted this sacrifice in her heart as well as upon her lips. She knew a passing pride in her renunciation. Even in her childhood she had been circumspect of soul, and now once more she put temptation from her. For, standing upon the lonely moor, she said in a resolute voice :

' The generosity and the sacrifice have been God's. I have tried to be worthy. And yet . . . and yet ! '

The sky was starless and grey with mist from the sea. Anna went on her way. Now her step was firm and her head lifted so that her tears would not fall.

She entered the living-room at Penmur where the family was sitting. Armandine came to meet her :

' Did you see Gildas, Aunt Anna ? '

' I saw the trap going to the station—that's all.'

' What a pity ! He told us such tales about the war, and we gave him two knapsacks of food to take back, his own and Pol's old one that Denise found. He looked so funny with them under his cloak.'

Denise, distressed by memories of her husband, broke in :

' Be quiet now, children ! '

The cloth was laid. Marie Maguern went over to her husband, who stood alone at the end of the room.

' I shouldn't say any more to-night about Gildas, if I were you, Jean-Guillaume. The way you've been going on, you'll lose your chance of Paradise. Try to see that just now he's not in the mood to be at home and that he couldn't stay any longer.'

Jean-Guillaume shrugged his shoulders with impatience, but said nothing.

At their meal Anna could take no more than a little soup. The old woman, seeing how she felt, drew the girl aside and said :

' Don't bother about the clearing up to-night, Anna. As soon as the boys are gone, be off to bed. You are tired out.'

CHAPTER XIII

CHÂTILLON COLLEGE

GILDAS spent a week at Châtillon-sur-Sèvre, a small town built upon a bleak hill in the wooded part of the Vendée. The country around, the ceaseless rain, did not interest him, but only the college itself, where, if he survived the war, he might hope to complete the short course necessary for his admission to the Great Seminary. There was a ferment in his spirit come of the fighting at the front, of talks in the trenches, of his consciousness of a future not yet revealed and of this first acquaintance with a seminarist's life.

The crowded college was filled with a strange peace. Its buildings consisted of two houses on opposite sides of a road, linked by an underground passage. In the larger house were the usual classrooms and dormitories, while the few professors whom the war had left at the college also had their quarters there. Most of these were old men and all of them overworked by their duties during the day and by their own necessary studies at night.

The seminarists themselves fell into two strangely contrasting groups. There were only the very young boys, and the men from the Army who were eight, twelve or even twenty years older. The war had taken thirteen in all from their desks to the dug-outs, and of the thirteen seven had been killed already. Their example was kept steadily before the young boys, whose hearts responded to its tragic nobility.

Except in this they were not more thoughtful than their kind. They ran and shouted : they had all the fun and warm-heartedness and idealism of youth. Their boisterous games in the college playground sent the many birds which lived in the trees of its quiet quadrangle scattering over the terraced gardens and into the wooded park beyond at the sound of the recreation bell, to return when it was over and the court was quiet. This sudden silence and strange peace after the babel of recreation moved Gildas greatly, coming as he had from life in barracks and trenches. Here at Châtillon he found a gentler discipline and, in the boys, seriousness at the thought of their future priesthood, early yearnings after perfection and the beginnings of self-mastery.

He had no sooner asked for hospitality than he was given a room and books to read. He was taken in charge by one of the oldest of the college professors, who had been obliged to undertake lessons in mathematics and geography in addition to his usual junior class work. Gildas and he went by the underground passage beneath the street, and climbed the hill to the unpretentious presbytery adjoining the church on the crest.

' I expect you'd like to tell me about yourself, my dear fellow,' the old man said with the friendly informality which he showed to all his pupils.

They had an intimate talk as they walked in the Superior's garden among the rows of vegetables and under the wall overgrown with grasses. To the country boy, with his profound religious instinct and his dream of consecration and future apostolate, the conversation

was enthralling. It rambled from subject to subject, as
Gildas asked his ingenuous questions and told his simple
stories of life at Penmur. At times he became timid and
silent, abashed at the liberty he had taken. Then the
professor, as was his habit, would rub his hands and
smile, good-humoured wrinkles showing at the corners
of his eyes and mouth. For in Gildas he saw himself
again as a young man. His great experience gave him a
clear perception of the boy's soul. His voice was quiet
and his words were wise ; for long meditation had given
him verbal skill equalling his essential goodness.

He had none of the impetuosity of an imaginative man
who sees only the heights : the length of the road and its
obstacles were well known to him. He was a worthy
guide to spiritual perfection ; he was fair-minded and
sympathetic towards the young man's vocation and the
perplexities which it had brought him. Like Gildas he
had come from the country. Beneath his polish which
education had brought, the young soldier recognised a
spirit as simple and as healthy as his own. At the end
of the week the two had become great friends, and both
were grieved at parting. In their last intimate talk at
the bottom of the garden the old man had asked : ' Will
you come back here to finish your studies ? '

' How long will that take ? '

' At least two years. Then you'll go on to the big
seminary at Poitiers. And when you've finished
there . . .'

' You take my breath away.'

' Well, time's short. Now—when you've finished
there, do you wish to be a priest in the country ? '

' I think I do. You see, I was born there.'

' Well, aren't you sure ? You must have thought of

the future. We all do when we're young. It's only old men like myself who live in the past. What is it you're not sure about ? '

' Well, father, I was just going to say . . .' He stopped there. The priest laughed and said : ' Well, go on ! '

' I feel I'd like to do works of love.'

The other laughed again, so loudly this time that he brought the Superior to his window.

' Whatever kind of priest you are, you'll always find works of love to be done.'

Becoming serious, he looked intently at Gildas to assure himself that the boy was neither hurt nor embarrassed, and that he would keep inviolate in his soul his liking for ' works of love.'

' You're right, Gildas. God delights in works of love. When the time comes, he'll reveal to you where there is most need in the world, and you'll be sent.'

' Yes, father ; I hope so.'

' I shall be glad to see that day.'

The priest drew his silver watch from his cassock pocket.

' You'll have to hurry. Run and say good-bye to the Superior. Don't forget your knapsacks. I've put a bottle of wine in one of them. We must be off to the station. I am coming with you.'

Gildas left him there, rubbing his cold hands as he did so often.

Gildas had gone on leave from S. Ouen in the Aube. He found his unit, his friends and the chaplain in the same quarters on his return. He started his Latin lessons again, but they were soon to end.

During that March, after thirty-two months of fighting, war weariness was extreme. Behind their barbed-wire entanglements France and Germany waged a war of attrition. The French were preparing for an offensive in April. Out of the trenches, the men trained rather than rested. These early months in the spring of 1917 were months of hardship for Gildas Maguern and his companions. In April they went back to the trenches. Near Rheims on the 16th they took part, with the Russians, in the offensive which, it was hoped, would finish the war. The attack completely failed; for details of it had been found beforehand by the enemy on the body of a dead officer. Until the end of July the regiment had to hold the dangerous sector in front of the powerful fort of Brimont whose guns killed many of its men.

During the last weeks a reconnoitring party was sent out to examine a nest of machine-guns believed to be abandoned. By the light of a star-shell the Germans saw the five volunteers who crept forward. Shells burst and bullets whistled. Gildas, peering over the parapet next to a lookout, saw dim shadows of men running, and hurried down the trench to the point opposite the gap in the barbed wire. He had taken only a few steps when someone came towards him with arms waving, calling out: ' Lanio's been hit. Listen to him shouting.'

' I'll go,' said Gildas.

Leading the others, he ran down the winding trench. Opposite the gap, he saw three shadows, two men carrying a third. A group of men had soon collected. Voices were heard:

' It's the chaplain—he's killed ! It can't be ! '

They were all eager to help; for the chaplain had been greatly loved. But the stretcher-bearers and the officer appeared, and shouted to the men to make way for them.

Gildas saw for a brief moment his friend's face, chalk-white but for the blood streaming between his eyes. A wound the whole length of his leg showed through his torn cassock, from which the blood poured down upon the duck-boards, as often drenched by this kind of rain as by the other.

Gildas, like many of his comrades, did not sleep that night. They talked of the chaplain:

'He's dead, that's certain. As usual he was the first to climb over when Lanio had to be fetched in. He was over before we could stop him. He didn't try to hide. The Boches fired at him, but a shell got both of them in the end when he was seeing to Lanio. What a good chap he was! And brave!'

Gildas found himself thinking as he lay in his shelter: 'We at least are armed, but he went under fire without even a walking-stick, to do his works of love.'

On the following morning he learned that the chaplain had lost an eye, while his body was so shattered that he was not expected to live the day.

Weeks passed. The exhausted regiment was ordered to a rest camp in Parroy Forest in Lorraine. The men thought it strange to see so many growing and un-damaged trees. They stayed there some time, until each company was brought up to its full strength. At the end of the summer Gildas wrote home to say that the chaplain had been seriously wounded near Berry-aux-Bac on July 27. For two months he had been near Epernay.

He must by this time be convalescing; for they had given him a glass eye and crutches.

He finished : ' Even if he gets better, we shall not see him again. If he tried to ride, he would not be able to stay in the saddle. Everybody wishes he were back—especially me. My grammar is still in my knapsack, but I never open it. It's had the corner taken off by a shell-splinter, but it saved my life. I am very well both in mind and body.'

His mother, having read the letter, went to find Jean-Guillaume. He was in the stable giving lucern to the cattle :

' Here's another letter from the boy.'

From the stable door she read it to him, while from his uplifted fork the lucern fell about him.

She finished reading. As he turned to the cattle, Jean-Guillaume's only comment was :

' I don't wish anyone harm, but now the chaplain's gone, I can't help thinking that the boy may change his mind and be a bit more reasonable.'

' There's not much hope of that, seeing he's your son. How often do you change your mind ? And there's even less chance as he's in the right.'

She returned to the house, which latterly she rarely left.

In the spring of 1918 when Foch was Commander-in-Chief, the 9th Corps was put under General Maugin. The men were worthy of such a leader. Fierce fighting went on without a break between the Oise and the Marne. The Germans began to waver ; the French took back village after village. The Hindenburg line was attacked and broken. Laon was assaulted and captured. As

the occupied territory was freed and trench warfare
changed to open fighting, there was unceasing talk
among the men of the advance to the Rhine.

During these months, when his unit was constantly
moving forward, Gildas wrote only postcards to Penmur.
They said merely that he was alive and well. Once only,
full of joy at the thought of victory, he wrote home
proudly as so many were doing at that time :

' We're on top. The war will soon be over. Everywhere they are on the run. I won't write any more now
except to say that I am keeping to my idea. My love
to you all.'

Anna was present when this letter was read. To hide
her emotion from the family, who had all come into
shelter from the pouring rain, she went out to the stable
through the boys' room.

The scattered clouds of the morning had brought in
their train a closed dark curtain through which no light
escaped. Sheets of rain fell continuously. Streams of
dirty water splashed over the pebbles in the farmyard
and ran down to the pool, carrying with it heaps of
manure. Not a single beast stirred from its shelter ;
all the cattle had been brought in. The dry, cracked
earth was saturated by the rain, its clefts filled with
swollen roots and clods.

At the far end of the stable, Anna stood on the flags
and leaned against the wall, sick at heart. For until
now she had not entirely given up hope. Despite her
renunciation of home, husband, and children she had
clung in secret to the belief that she might be relieved
of her obligation. But that day's letter had destroyed
this belief. Fighting back tears, she tried to summon the
courage to seek out Jean-Guillaume, whom she had seen

cross the yard and go into the shed, and now heard sawing in the shed. Covering her head with her skirt, she at last opened the stable door abruptly and splashed through the yard along the hedge which separated it from the cliff. The shed was a primitive building near the cliff. Four wooden uprights supported the great tiled roof : tiles and uprights were at least a hundred years old. The roof itself was covered with lichens and moss whose greys and silvers shone against the green of the trees, making the roof seem in the distance merely a tall patch of heather. Four generations of Maguerns had worked there. Jean-Guillaume in his turn was sawing logs and cutting up fine wood for the house. He had no liking for this work, which Denise had demanded he should do, and he was glad to rest when he saw his niece.

From the girl's grave manner and half-fearful eyes he guessed that her business was urgent. ' What is it, Anna ? ' he asked, putting down his saw.

' Uncle, I want more money.'

At once he was on his guard :

' More money ! You're all alike. Where do you think I'm to get it from ? '

' This is the first time I've ever asked.'

' You know I've always paid you a fair wage and more. Haven't you always been well fed and clothed with a good roof over your head ? '

' I've nothing to say against all that.'

' You've had a hundred and thirty francs a year when lots of the farmers only give a hundred and twenty.'

' Yes, I know.'

' And you've had the stuff for your dress, three yards

of ordinary and three yards of good, like we agreed—haven't you now ? '

' Yes.'

' And I set a new example round here in giving the servant a sheep for herself. You sold the wool at a good price, to say nothing of the two lambs.'

' That's true.'

' What about the three rows of potatoes you've had from the best part of the field ? '

' I know, uncle.'

After a moment's silence, looking her full in the face he went on :

' And you never even had to dig the potatoes when Gildas was here. He always did it for you.'

Unable to meet his gaze she turned from him, her grief temporarily mastering her. He continued :

' You know very well I have to work three farms. There's those two women I help now that their men are away.'

' That's a work of love, uncle, if ever there was.'

' Well, I haven't got the money, so I can't give it to you.'

He looked first at the stormy pool and then back to the girl's face. He was puzzled by her persistence ; for until to-day she had been content with her wages.

' Is it your velvet dress you've got to pay for ? '

' I can't tell you, uncle.'

' Well, I never see you in it these days.'

' It's no good thinking about finery in war-time.'

He thought for a moment, and then picked up a log : his anger showed itself in his vigorous sawing.

' You can't have it, Anna. The most I can give you

is another row of potatoes. But it won't be in the best part this time.'

'Thank you, uncle.'

'You needn't thank me, because I grudge it to you.'

CHAPTER XIV

TWO HUNDRED FRANCS

As she went back to the house Anna thought : ' The row of potatoes will help anyway, especially when they're as good as this year's in Old Cross Field. But it will be September or October before they're dug and some time after that before they're sold. And they don't pay at once. I'd like to be able to send the fees for Gildas, so that they won't be able to say in the Vendée : " Is Jean-Guillaume so hard up that he can't find six hundred francs ? "—I know ! I'll ask a few of my friends to help. They won't tell, and Gildas will never find out. Now, let me think ! First there's Marguerite Voilier.'

The next day Anna hurried through her household tasks and at sunset was free for the evening. She changed her clogs for her Sunday shoes, and took the familiar path over the fields to Marguerite Voilier's house.

In the evening light the widow sat by her window mending a Muzillac head-dress.

' Haven't you any glasses, Marguerite ? ' Anna said.

' My sight is still good, God be thanked, at least in the daylight. Have you come to ask me something ? '

' Yes, can you help me ? I've got to get six hundred francs.'

184

' For yourself ? '

' Oh, no ! '

' I suppose it's for Gildas, then ? '

' Yes, it's for him. So that his fees can all be paid before he goes to Châtillon College.'

' It's settled that he's going then ? '

' As soon as the war's over. In his letter to-day he said we're winning.'

' That's good news. Well, wait a minute ! '

She straightened the thick folds of her black dress as she rose quickly and crossed to a cupboard opposite the window. Standing on tiptoe, she searched in a drawer, finally taking down a box that rattled in her hand. After she had tidied the drawer, she came towards the girl holding something that gleamed dully.

' Two louis, Anna ! From before the war. I've been keeping them for a rainy day—not that I have anything else much. But to give Brittany one more priest I'll let you have them gladly.'

' Oh, what a lot, Aunt Marguerite ! ' Anna exclaimed as she took the gold coins. ' How much are they worth now ? '

' I have no idea. Perhaps thirty francs.'

' I'll ask the solicitor or the notary in Muzillac. But thank you. You'll have your reward in heaven.'

The words recalled to the old woman the meditations which filled her hours of solitude. She murmured :

' That's all we're here for—at least, so I think.' Filled with sudden joy, she went on : ' When I stand before God, do you know what I shall say to him ? '

' What, Aunt Marguerite ? '

' I shall say, " Kiss me, Lord ! " '

They laughed happily together. Quickly their

laughter changed to gravity, and in a moment more they had regained their usual solemnity.

' Some griefs have their beauty,' the old woman said, ' and later bring their blessing. Where are you off to now, Anna ? '

' To the town. I know who to go and see. I thought I'd come to you first, and I've been very lucky.'

' Well, it's a fine evening for you, but it will be dark soon.'

Anna left the house and walked over the fields to Muzillac. She called on neither the solicitor nor the notary. Her only visit was to an old woman who, though retired, sometimes acted as sick-nurse. She said to Anna :

' You are asking me to help your boy who doesn't want you any longer ? '

' No, Florentine ! I'm asking you to help God—for God wants him.'

The woman's heart was touched by this answer, worthy of France herself.

' It's grand work you're doing, Anna. You know I'm not rich, but here's three francs. If you'll be guided by me, you won't go to too many people. I understand, but many wouldn't.'

' But it's those people Gildas will have to help.'

Anna said good-bye. Although she was glad at heart, she had not the courage to call upon Rosalie Menez who lived close by. She went out into the darkness again, thinking, ' Still more than five hundred francs to get ! It's going to be a long, hard job.'

She went next to the old man who used to work the mill which now stood idle at Penmur Pool. They stood at the bank by the pool, which broadened out here after passing through a gorge, their two figures reflected in the water, that was covered in floating leaves. The roar of the water had left him very deaf, and Anna had to shout to explain her mission, but at last he understood, and in his response proved generous.

Sunday after Sunday the girl made similar expeditions into the country. Yet on that Monday when the bells rang for the Armistice, she was still far short of the necessary sum. Anna imagined that in a short while Gildas would be home. Although he often wrote short affectionate letters to the farm, none of them spoke of the future. There was one means left to her of making up the amount of Gildas' fees. She thought of it constantly, and as constantly shrank from it.

On the Sunday following the Armistice, as she had heard of no further letter from Gildas, she came to her decision. After Mass her friends of whom she enquired told her that Valentine could be found at home in the early evening. Anna was free about the same time. In the autumn evening, which seemed more like spring than autumn, Anna went to visit her. The light was soft, the sky cloudless, a summer fragrance was in the air. Against the clear sky every leaf and twig showed plain. From Coléno a child's voice filled the peaceful Sunday silence with its music.

Before she started, she had waited in the living-room until all had gone—Armandine had been the last to leave on some small errand to the loft. With a beating heart Anna opened the chest in which she kept her clothes and her embroidered head-dresses. Beneath the neat folds of her best dress was the white napkin into which she had wrapped and pinned the cherry-coloured velvet.

Memories of that past Christmas time came back to her. She thought of Gildas for whose delight she had worn the apron. He was lost to her now—the apron remained. She took it into her arms still in its white wrapping. As though it were a child, she pressed it to her. She dared not unwrap it, lest her courage should fail. Softly she said good-bye to it. Taking a covered wicker egg-basket, she slipped the white package into it and, smoothing it gently, left the house.

She remembered that she had worn the dress once only. Yet now she was about to offer it to Valentine whose rich fiancé, the tall Trémoir, badly wounded in the war, was already home. Anna recited to herself the little speech with which she would approach Valentine : ' There's no need to unwrap it. It's just as it was when I wore it that Christmas two years ago. You saw it after Mass. Ever since I've kept it wrapped away in the chest. Never mind about the napkin now. You can let me have it when you're passing, some time.'

The basket was light upon her arm, but her heart grew increasingly heavy, as she neared the farm by the sea where Valentine lived. It would be hard to smile as she made her offer. Yet there are some griefs that must be kept hidden.

Anna went along the main road. Two cars passed her, tearing along to Vannes. Then she turned into the quiet lanes and came within sight of the sea sparkling through the trees. The bells pealing for Benediction added to the peace of the afternoon. She hurried to be sure of finding Valentine before the rest of the family returned from church.

She climbed the last stile and crossed the low meadow

whose gate opened upon the road leading to the farm. It was a modern house built upon three sides of a well-kept farm-yard.

Anna paused on the doorstep to summon courage. All was still. As she softly knocked three times, she heard footsteps that seemed to die away. Finally a voice said : ' Come in ! '

Valentine was standing in the living-room. Although in the country Sunday is the day for writing letters, there was neither writing paper nor ink upon the oak table. She saw that near Valentine's chair a second chair was set, and guessed that it was Trémoir's and that the footsteps she had heard had been his. Putting down her basket on the end of the table, she crossed to Valentine who greeted her :

' Good afternoon, Anna. I didn't expect you.'

' That's plain enough. You had a visitor already, hadn't you ? ' she said, glancing at the empty chair.

Valentine was in no way confused ; for it was known that she was engaged.

' Yes, he was with me, when we heard your knock. We didn't know who it was. I expect he's outside somewhere. Why have you brought a basket ? You can't want eggs or a chicken—you've plenty at Penmur.' She finished with a merry laugh.

Her complexion and her figure were good. Her eyes sparkled beneath her chestnut hair. Not so tall as Anna, she had the easy speech and gestures of the well-to-do ; while her expression told of happiness as well as prosperity.

' Sit down, Anna.'

But Anna merely leaned against the table, her hands

hanging limply. Her eyes were downcast and grief had put wrinkles about her mouth. She said :

' You know, Valentine, that my cousin Gildas will soon be starting his studies at the College . . . ? '

The other girl suppressed an involuntary smile.

' Yes, I've heard. They tell me you've been very brave about it.'

' I don't know about being brave. Gildas would never have left me except for his vocation. So I must try to get the money to pay for his fees.'

' What a Christian you are, Anna ! '

' So are you. That's why I've come to see if you will help.'

' I'll do what I can.' She had taken a step towards the other room, when Anna broke in :

' No, Valentine, I haven't come to beg, but I've come to see if . . . if you'll buy my embroidered velvet apron. I've only worn it once and . . . I'll never wear it again.'

Anna took the packet from her basket and gave it to Valentine, who had become suddenly serious.

' It's the best thing I've got, Valentine. It'll bring you a blessing if you buy it.'

The pins fell upon the table as Valentine opened the napkin and took out the cherry-coloured apron.

' Oh, how lovely ! I remember how beautiful you looked that day. But what's the matter with you— you've gone so pale ? What are you looking at ? Oh, it's only Trémoir coming back.'

She laughed as she waved her fiancé imperiously away. He had gently opened the door and now stood on the threshold. The gay good humour and youthful coquetry with which she dismissed him contrasted strangely with Anna's gravity, Trémoir, who had lost an arm in the war, was one of the most handsome men in the parish. As he stood there in the half-dusk saluting the girl, he looked the smart soldier he had been. Anna saw that he had a fair moustache and blue eyes and that his bearing was resolute. Valentine laughed again :

' No need to go away, silly ! We're not frightened by you. This is Anna—she's heard about you already. She has come to sell me her lovely velvet apron.'

With his swinging stride he came into the room. He was dressed in smart town clothes and was plainly very much at home in that house. A good-natured man, he was fond of joking. With a smile he fingered the dress, and turning to Anna said :

' Couldn't you put it on, mademoiselle ? We shall then be able to see what it's like. I'm sure you must look very pretty in it.'

Trémoir knew nothing of the girl's story ; for he had not long been back from the war and his home was not in the parish. With amazement he saw her shrink away, hands before her face, saying :

' I can't—I can't bear to put it on again.'

Valentine caught the apron from him and whispered :

' Stop, Trémoir, stop ! She's only worn it once, but it didn't help her. Don't bother her ; she's so upset.'

Aloud she said : ' I'll try it on.'

The other two watched her, as she folded the rich velvet about her, fastening it with pins.

' You do look lovely ! ' Trémoir said, as he started forward, intending to kiss her.

' Please don't ! Not while Anna's here—you don't understand ! '

' My luck's out,' he murmured. ' Nothing I can say is right.'

Involuntarily they looked at Anna leaning listlessly against the bread-bin by the wall, her hands behind her back. With her white face and her staring tearless eyes she might well have been a royalist rebel of the Vendée, waiting to be shot and knowing escape to be impossible. To her this simple sale of a velvet apron was almost as tragical. Wistfully she saw how happy they were in each other, and waited till they should remember her.

Bending her head with a graceful movement, Valentine noticed a tiny stain at the corner of the apron.

' Look, Anna ! You didn't say it was stained. Was it rain ? '

Trémoir saw Anna shake her head slowly and sadly. Although he knew nothing of her story, he guessed at once that a tear had caused the stain. He turned to Valentine, saying gruffly :

' Give her the money. She's terribly upset. She'll be better away from here. It doesn't matter about the stain. I'll give you a gold brooch to wear over that. Do pay her ! '

Valentine at once looked serious. For this was a matter of business.

' Will you take two hundred francs ? It isn't new, you know.'

' Yes, if you think that's fair. I don't want to haggle,' said Anna tonelessly.

Anna left the farm soon afterwards. Her basket

was empty, but she had two hundred francs in her pocket.

The sky was still serene. From the distant beach at Billiers Anna could hear the faint moaning of the sea. It might well have been the sorrow in her own heart made articulate.

CHAPTER XV

THE GREY STOCKINGS

AT the end of the year the older men began to come home. Gildas was one of the younger soldiers sent to Mainz in the German provinces occupied under the terms of the Armistice. They understood that discipline must be stern in this conquered city, for they knew they were perpetually watched by a hostile people embittered by defeat. Their officers impressed on them that each one of them was a representative of his country, and most of the soldiers, among them Gildas, played their unenviable part honourably. Now that they were at peace they all felt more secure about their futures, and were able to make friends with their comrades from other battalions.

He had been only a month in the Rhineland when he began to study Latin once more. He still had his old grammar with him. From shops in the town he bought the Latin classics, but the German notes to these made them of no great use to him, and so he managed to get hold of editions published in Paris. Fortunately, in the meantime he had made a friend of a professor from Paris, Jean-Louis Bolsenne, the son of a well-off middle-class family. This brilliant scholar came from the seminary of Issy and, like the chaplain, had been wounded at

Berry-au-Bac. In Gildas he perceived a soul of great strength, a born ploughman of the human heart.

At the end of September 1919, both men were discharged from the Army. They travelled as far as Paris together. Before they parted, Jean Bolsenne said :

' Gildas, I'll tell you what I've dreamed of your doing, though I doubt if you'll find it possible. Yet there's no harm in telling you.'

' Yes ? '

' Well, after I've finished at the seminary, I'm going as a novice to the house at Clichy of Notre-Dame-Auxiliatrice where priests train for " Zone " mission work.'

' I'd like that too.'

' They are called " Sons of Charity." '

' That's a noble name.'

' They are pledged to take subordinate posts as parish priests or curates in the working-class quarters of Paris or the big industrial towns, and to change their parish if it's not a poor one.'

' Is there any reason why I can't come too ? '

' You haven't the time. You have to do a year's probation. But you can be a Zone priest without going to Clichy. As you are nearly twenty-four, Gildas, it would be far better to go to Châtillon which you know already. And you'll get fit again in the air of the Vendée. Two years will be long enough if you go on working as you're doing now. Then you can come to Issy. I shall be nearly leaving then, and we'll have a little time together.'

' I'll do anything you like.'

' Just one thing more. I've arranged that you can stay with my parents for a few days if you like. After that

I'll take you round to a religious house near there, where you can make a fairly long retreat before you begin your new life.'

At the beginning of October Gildas began a retreat lasting ten days. From the house on the hill of Athis-Mons he wrote to his mother :

' Dear Mother, my watch on the Rhine is over, and I am back in France. We've got the Alsace frontier settled. I shall be here in Paris for over a week. This will give me time to pray and to meditate and to examine my soul, as I need to do before I take this step. Try to understand me, mother, when I say I am going straight to Châtillon. I may falter if I come back to Penmur, but it will be hard not to see you again. Hard but best—as you often used to say. Forgive me. Though I'm learning new lessons now, I shall never forget your own. Good-bye for the present, mother.'

At Penmur Marie Maguern gave the letter to Jean-Guillaume. Handing it back, he said :

' How shall we manage now with him lost to us and Ange doing his service ? There's only Alexis.'

His wife was busy mending a pair of black stockings. In the poor light she strained her eyes. Coming across to her Jean-Guillaume shook his head, saying :

' You're crying.'

' No more than yesterday.'

' Is it because of what I said about Gildas ? He would have been here now, if you hadn't backed him up.'

He went away muttering. The old woman called shrilly after him :

' Crying ? I never used to, but I could now. Stupid !

You don't understand me or the boy. Men can't make sacrifices. All they can do is fight.'

After a moment she murmured to herself : ' Crying ! It was only the black wool. I'll rest my eyes a bit, and darn some grey ones.'

She got up and went to look for the grey wool.

CHAPTER XVI

CALLED LATE

AT twenty past nine on the evening of October 11, 1919, Gildas, still wearing his uniform, reached Châtillon-sur-Sèvre. All he possessed was a shaving set and tooth brush, a few letters, picture postcards of Mainz and Paris and the Latin grammar which he carried in his knapsack.

Consciousness of his poverty made him heavy-hearted. He was about to become dependent on others for everything—board and lodging, books and tuition. It was true that two years before the Superior had told him curtly that he need have no fear about that, and then had dismissed the subject. Yet he could not afford this generosity, Gildas was convinced, and it irked his Breton pride to think of a Maguern in such a position.

He turned from the main Poitiers road into the steep Rue de la Poste, at the top of which was the clerical school, the square, the church, and the Superior's garden and house, which was entered through the ancient gateway of the old abbey.

He rang. It was Father Courtin, the Superior himself, who answered. He had been warned of Gildas' arrival by a postcard, and was waiting for him. Once more Gildas saw the old priest with his broad brow, his weary face, his keen and shining eyes with their thick lashes. He gave Gildas no smile ; for the exercise of authority during fifty years had left his face stern. Something, nevertheless, in his silent welcome suggested that this sternness hid true simplicity of heart.

' You're a little late, aren't you, Gildas Maguern ? '

' Yes, father ; the train was ten minutes behind.'

' I see. Your luggage is at the station, I suppose ?'

Flushing, the boy drew the dog-eared textbook from his knapsack, and said :

' This is all I've brought back.'

The old man looked at the title :

' We don't use that here, but I will give you a little one that I've written.'

' As I told you last year, father, my parents have money but I have none. I'm writing to my mother, and perhaps she will send me some. I'm just a poor soldier now.'

' Your mother has done so already. Two days ago she sent quite a lot.'

' I'm glad about that, father. I expected she'd send a little. It's very hard not to have enough to pay for board and lodging.'

As they crossed the presbytery yard with its scent of heliotrope, the Superior laughed and, forgetting his usual gravity, said :

' There's no need to worry. Your board and lodging is paid for a full year. The six hundred francs——'

Gildas started. ' My father must have sent that,' he said.

' I don't think so. Let me see ! It was a Mme Voilier who sent the money order.'

The Superior, perceiving though not understanding the

young man's emotion, put his hand on his arm. His voice was low as he said :

' You'll have other proof later on of the sacrifices Christians make to help give God a priest. For they know what a noble vocation it is ! For your part, you must be proud that one day you will intercede for them. Come along, my boy ! The others have already had supper and gone to their dormitory. I'll introduce you to two of the staff who are still here.'

They went into the house. After they had greeted him, Gildas went by the underground passage to the college and to his white bed at the far end of the dormitory, where several pairs of eyes watched the new-comer. Tired with his journey, he was soon asleep. When he awoke it was Sunday morning. After a quick cold bath he dressed and went down the winding stairs. With the others he went to first Mass, and after break-fast to his studies. About ten o'clock he put on his red cassock, and took his place in the choir of the parish church. In all the crowded congregation there was no familiar face. He spent the free time before the midday meal in unpacking a parcel from his mother. He changed into a suit of civilian clothes and put away his other belongings into a locker that he had been given. He asked the college housekeeper about certain necessary alterations to those clothes, which he had worn three years before.

He paid a visit to the office, and by dinner-time had been formally enrolled at the college. At recreation he was surrounded by the other students and was the object of many curious glances and questions. There was a certain shyness of him as a man who had seen the horrors of war and had come near to death, and his

reticence left their curiosity largely unsatisfied. Even
his clothes seemed strange in their eyes : he wore an
old Sunday suit that was rather short on him, since it
had been made for him before the war. His waistcoat
and jacket were of a thick black cloth with grey stripes,
while he carried a new felt hat. When he had found this
in the parcel, Gildas had wondered who had bought it for
him. Plainly neither his father nor Alexis had chosen
it ; it must have been a woman—but who ? He was
brought to himself by the laughing voice of one of the
smallest boys there, an intelligent curly-headed youngster
who said amid the laughter of his companions : ' You're
as tall as a poplar ! Will you drill us ? Tell us about
the fighting. You come from Brittany, don't you ?
Do you speak Breton ? Are you really in the sixth ?
That's where we are.'

Gildas' only reply was to put on his hat and to stride
past them frowning. He made his way to an old elm
planted in a paved square at the bottom of the yard, and
leaning against it looked over the country-side beyond
the terraced slopes of the town. Utterly absorbed, he
neither heard nor saw the mob of shouting boys. So
S. Sebastian has often been painted, as he stood waiting
for the shafts to fly.

His mind was a tumult of thought and emotion. The
yard, the terraced houses, the wide expanse of park, the
meadows and great woods beyond—all seemed to join
in the question which he asked himself : ' What am I
doing here ? What have I in common with these kids
after years with men in the trenches ? How can I grind
away with boys in the lowest classes all to learn words in a
dead tongue ? . . . I'd sooner shout to the beasts in
Penmur. . . . It'll take seven years, and even then what

sort of scholar shall I be ? It was a different story at home. I knew how to handle the plough—but when it's the pen . . . I can't stand this ! For three years I did my bit in the trenches, and then for another one on the Rhine. That was a man's work if you like. But I'll never get used to this—it's too late in the day. I'll write home to my mother. She'll be grieved ; so shall I. Yes, it's too late. I can't be penned up here. Father won't want explanations, poor old man ! He'll be glad enough to have me back. He's only got Alexis to help with the work this autumn. I'll go back.'

The boys had gone on with their games. They had lost interest in the tall new-comer and his dreamy staring. The master in charge had understanding enough to guess how it was with Gildas. He knew that anything that he might say then would merely irritate the boy. Later, he would take him aside and express his sympathy.

As he watched the sky with its white wisps of cloud, memories continued to haunt Gildas. Once more he saw Penmur and the cliffs of the pool ; the living-room with the three box-beds ; the team of brown oxen ; his sister Armandine, who at fifteen must be a fine girl. Thoughts of Anna came into his mind. He saw her as he remembered her on that Christmas day before he joined the Army ; once more she sat beside him in the waggon-ette. He could picture every detail of her dress ; the diadem with its embroidered stars ; the fine chain of her locket ; the cloak which she wore, and her unhappy face as she fastened its clasps, hiding the velvet dress.

For a moment this vision of her was startlingly clear. At the next it was gone. Suddenly he realised that these pictures were a temptation sent to him.

' Help me, O God ! I can stand no more.'

He had spoken aloud. Raising himself, he looked across at the boys. A man of medium height with a black beard was coming towards the elm tree. When he spoke in his friendly voice, Gildas guessed him to be one of the older students :

' I'm le Barbu. At three when we go for our walk come along with me and Berceau. He's a good sort. We're older than the rest, and we shall get on together.'

Gildas nodded his thanks. Once more he fell into his old absorption. Until the bell rang, he stood staring at the sky. When they went to the classrooms, his companions noticed that he kept his right hand in his pocket. They guessed his rosary was there.

After Vespers they walked in file towards the Poitiers road, the smallest boys in front, with a young priest in charge of them.

' Where are we going, father ? Into the Knights' Wood ? '

' Yes.'

' Are we going to the Big Oak ? Good ! There'll be squirrels.'

It was a fine day, and the boys were in high spirits. As they left the town, they talked and joked. Gildas walked between le Barbu and his friend Berceau. Le Barbu was well-named ; for he was the only student with a beard, and was burly, with gleaming black eyes. He wore gold ear-rings, probably an heirloom. Though in the classroom he found construing difficult, meditation and the way of sacrifice came easily to him. No boy in the seminary was more boisterous and gay than he. His home was in the heart of the country.

Jérôme Berceau had been a mechanic. During the

war this tall rough fellow had driven an armoured car,
and later an express on one of the great French lines.
Neither his boyhood nor his youth had in any way
served him as preparation for the priesthood. From
twelve to twenty he had not practised his religion.
Suddenly during the war a series of small incidents,
conversations and examples, each trifling in itself, had
converted him. His qualities were strangely mixed. He
was boisterous and practical ; he was a joker and a
mystic. He sang songs in several dialects ; talked with
assurance on any topic, and could act a part—a comic
part in particular—with ability and wit, although some
of these parts could certainly not have been played at
Châtillon. On his jacket he now wore a small Sacred
Heart badge.

Within a week his inventiveness and gift of leadership
had made him popular at the college. Whenever he
appeared in the playground, the boys crowded round
him, crying : ' Come on, Jérôme ! Play with us like you
did yesterday ! '

The three were near the end of the file. From the
stubble-fields came a faint perfume. Above them the
clouds drove in a white procession. Soon the men were
talking of the war, comparing experiences and exchang-
ing views. Jérôme and Gildas had been mentioned in
despatches. Their endurance and suffering in the past
quickened their growing friendship in the present.
Because of both past and present they were soon asking
each other the fundamental question : ' Why did you
come here ? ' It was Berceau who first asked Gildas,
as they climbed the steep hill leading to Knights'
Wood :

' The call first came to me, when I was a boy,' he

replied. ' But until a short time ago, I took no notice. That's all.'

Turning to le Barbu, the other continued :

' You come from round here, don't you ? What made you want to be a priest ? '

Le Barbu stroked his black beard, and after a moment's silence said with his ingenuous air :

' I had a good example set me.'

' Well, that's more than I had,' Berceau replied. ' But tell us, won't you ? '

' In our part of the country, and in my family especially, I had good examples set me all the time I was a boy. They made me feel I should never be satisfied unless I became a priest. But it took me a long time to make up my mind.'

The mechanic was silent for a moment or so. His manner suggested that with him it had been neither a secret call to his heart nor the force of example around him which had made him wish to give up the world. In his somewhat vulgar voice that he strove to improve he at length replied :

' Well, it's misery that made me think of it. I've seen no end at the works when I was an engineer ; in the coal-bunkers and stokeholds when I was at sea ; among the railway folk when I was a driver on the 1703. It sickened me. I wondered how I could help these people I worked with. You've no notion of the deluded ideas they're made to listen to, or what depths this leads them to. I broke away from them. Memories of my childhood came back to me, and I swore to help my comrades. For I was one of them. I decided to be a priest and go back to them. They'll recognise me by the way I shake my hand and the way I talk ; it makes you smile, but it won't them. I know I'm not very delicate. . . .'

Two hearty laughs answered this :

' Delicate ! You certainly aren't ! '

' There, you see ! But that won't matter much. The people will know I've got a good heart. I wonder if there have been any other workman-priests before ? '

As he looked away, a dreamy look came into his eyes. After a pause, he said :

' Anyway, you understand. No need to say any more.'

A youth from the row behind joined them. He was thin and appeared nervous ; his accent suggested that he came from the west or the south-west. He said :

' I heard what you were saying. I admire you for it, but all the same vocation comes in many ways. For instance, I went to a high school, and when I was nearly in the top form I had to think of my career. I asked myself, though I didn't dream where it would lead me, " When a man's free, what is the finest thing to choose to do ? " I thought it was logic that decided, but perhaps it was love. . . .'

After a moment he went on : ' You see, Jérôme Berceau, all kinds of things bring us here : I am proud to have met you ; you'll do good work for the missions.'

They shook hands. Berceau's only answer was a pleased smile.

The small boys in front began to flag ; for the hill grew steeper. Soon they came in sight of the Great Oak, great only in its girth. No green thing grew beneath the huge branches spreading fan-like from its trunk. This great tree was at the edge of Knights' Wood. Here the boys clamoured about their master, asking leave to run free in the wood. Soon they were shouting and climbing the trees. Gildas and his companions followed more slowly. Under the oak they were greeted with cries of : ' Hullo, Berceau ! Hullo, le Barbu ! Hullo, you Breton ! I say, Berceau, what shall we do ? '

' Let's go squirrel-hunting ! '

' Rather ! Let's start ! You and le Barbu can be the hounds. What are you going to do, Breton ? '

' I'm going to climb,' Gildas said, taking off his jacket. ' I mean to get some chestnuts.'

The men and a few of the older boys rested at the edge of the wood, waiting for the games to start. Taking a plug of tobacco from his pocket, Jérôme filled his pipe. For he had permission to smoke on these walks, provided that he gave passers-by no opportunity to say that everyone at Châtillon College smoked.

The priest in charge, who loved cigarettes but denied himself, walked in the smoke from Berceau's pipe that he might inhale its fragrance. He watched for the boys' return. Shortly he heard them shouting :

' There's one—a great black fellow, at the top of that chestnut tree. Come on, Berceau, le Barbu ! '

They all chased the leaping squirrels ; the boys' treble and the gruff voices of the men were heard as they imitated a dog's barking.

Before he slept that night, Gildas lay thinking of his talk with le Barbu and Berceau and the youth who had sought ' the finest thing a man can choose.' Resolutely he put from him his old haunting memories. In future he would discipline himself to think of his past merely in terms of years—twenty spent in the Brittany fields, three in the trenches, and one at his Latin on the banks of the Rhine. As his eyes closed, he murmured : ' O God !

help me to stay here ! You have your mysterious plan for me. Let me not destroy it ! '

Gildas was at Châtillon for two full years. There, after much hard honest work, he qualified for entrance to the Seminary at Issy.

In August 1920 he was sent for some weeks to assist the leader of a holiday retreat. The following year he was given leave to remain at Châtillon to work in the garden and on feast days to put flowers in the church. Like all candidates on the eve of their examination, he looked blankly at his books and grew depressed at the number of things which he seemed to have forgotten.

Finally, at the beginning of the autumn of 1921, he took a third-class ticket to Paris to enter upon one more stage of his probation.

CHAPTER XVII

AT ISSY-LES-MOULINEAUX

It was on a Wednesday early in October 1921 that Gildas Maguern became one of the four hundred seminarists at Issy-les-Moulineaux.

He soon became accustomed to the routine of this large and well-disciplined house. At Châtillon he had begun to know the value of time. Now he learned to use every second of the most precious of gifts, as the masters of ecclesiastical education had taught as far back as the seventeenth century. The seminary day began at five o'clock; at 5.30 was morning prayer and meditation; Mass at 6.15; sweeping of rooms at 7.5. . . .

No one was more conscientious than Gildas in keeping to the rules. If at a quarter to twelve when private study finished he was in the middle of writing a word, he at once stopped. He became as thrifty of time as his forefathers had been of money. He found delight in silence partly because it was a rule of the house, and partly because he knew that when his work began there would be all too little time for solitude and reflection. Yet private study was not easy for him. He preferred the stimulus of lectures. In philosophy his imperfect knowledge of Latin was a handicap; while in his case especially abstract thought was a weariness. He was not wholly happy in his life with this crowd of young Parisians from whom he was divided, and sometimes even alienated, by differences in family, education, wealth, and even manner of speech.

The short morning break of a quarter of an hour was taken behind the high building of the seminary under the lime trees and the chapel. Gildas found the customary strolling among the flower beds to be insufficient exercise. At Penmur and at Châtillon he had taken more, but only during the war had his body's need been wholly satisfied. At the long break after lunch at half-past twelve, however, they left the garden for the extensive park with its two great avenues, its tennis court and its basket-ball ground which was reached through an underground passage across the road. Here Gildas showed himself brilliant at games and made many friends.

He made others for profounder reasons. Keeping careful watch over his tongue as the charity which daily grew within him bade him, he reserved certain days in the week for talk with the 'Peripatetics,' as he called them. It had required effort on his part to join them for the first time as they strolled laughing beneath the two avenues of Lorette and S. John. The cassocks which most of them wore made him feel self-conscious in his own ill-fitting suit, which had grown shabby at Châtillon. He felt doubtful of his welcome, sure that his rawness was still apparent. Despite the friendliness with which he was received, it was some time before he lost his first timidity. Many of the seminarists came from old families, or had rich and cultured connections. Others were ex-officers from the Navy or Army, whose vocation, coming to them during the war, had thrown them into this new campaign for the souls of men. There was even a grey-haired colonel among them. It was such men as

these who greeted Gildas warmly. He quickly made
friends with several of them. Although they were somewhat amused by his ingenuousness, they were inspired
by his resolution, his purity, and his complete self-
effacement. He, on his part, envied their ease of manner,
and sought to imitate their urbanity, which was
attractive to him.

The Breton country boy absorbed the spirit of the
Sulpicians much more quickly than he mastered their
lectures in philosophy. His heart, his intellect, and his
early circumstances alike made it easy for him to understand the nobility of service and self-sacrifice. He saw
that his youth at Penmur and the life of those around
him taught him the same lesson which was the secret
of spiritual progress and true happiness. He tried to
express something of this in his letters to his mother :

' DEAR MOTHER,—

' It is now some months since I came here. More
and more I appreciate the beauty and the truth of the
teaching we are given. My studies are interesting
enough, but it is the motive behind which drives me to
use my thick head, which is about as promising as the
stoniest part of Old Cross Field. In my meditations I
mostly consider these two things : the past and the life
at Penmur which suited me so well ; the present and
how I can best make use of the precious gift made me
here. As it seems to me, I am free to make my own
choice from the abundant store of spiritual riches set
before me. Because you know so much of me, it won't
surprise you to know that what appeals to me most of
them all is what I used to see in you. In those early
days I did not realise how rich were the poor who have so

strong a faith as you, and all of us at home, thanks to
you.

'Now I understand, I think, the hidden meaning of
my love for Brittany. If I am to be worthy of it, I have
only to develop those virtues and those ways of life which
sons like me are taught by their mothers. Here we are
often told to love solitude and silence and self-forgetful-
ness ; we are exhorted to go into the world to toil at that
harvesting which is the glory of the Lord who provides
the seed for us to sow, making not ourselves but the good
we do shine in the world. You know how much I like
everything about me to be simple. At Penmur we were
born and grew up in such simplicity. Last night one of
the masters, a truly devout and wisely sympathetic man,
put this thought into words far more eloquent than mine.
He said : " *Nothing is more necessary to the world than
the Church ; nothing is more necessary to the Church
than its clergy ; nothing is more necessary to the clergy
than seminaries like Issy. For there holiness is instilled
into those who will celebrate the mystery of the Mass. I
can conceive nothing more noble than this humble and self-
sacrificing part that you are called upon to play. In a tree
the most assiduous cells are those of the leaves which
distribute the sap. They know the glory neither of flower
nor fruit, yet without them neither flower nor fruit would
have its being.*"

'You will understand, mother, how happy I am here.'

Marie Maguern did indeed understand. Each fort-
night, when she received a letter from Gildas, she would
read it first to herself and then aloud to her husband,
Denise, and Ange. Her discretion warned her not to
read it before Anna, for she wished to avoid hurting the

girl. Later, in some interlude of leisure, in the house or the loft, or in the orchard where the poultry were kept, she would read once more what Gildas had underlined in his letter.

Though her understanding often stumbled, she pondered these things in her heart. For she was not wholly a stranger to the more spiritual world in which her son moved. His faith was her faith. As the sense of his words grew plain, she walked the roads which Gildas followed, groping alone with the aid of her prayer-book, rosary, and sermons, and those many short wordless prayers which were prompted by difficulties in the day's work.

Almost always she herself sent the replies to these letters. It was her habit on Sundays to take a pen and the one small battered glass inkwell to be found in the house and to sit down laboriously to write. She found it harder work than the scouring of a big copper saucepan or the milking of four cows. Often she would call Denise to her aid, in her rare moments of leisure :

' I'm sending to Gildas—will you put down for me what I tell you ? Your writing is better than mine.'

Her daughter-in-law would settle herself at the table. After news had been given of each member of the family, the farm, and the parish, the letter would finish with what the old woman called *a little invitation*. ' Don't forget,' she said, ' that it is a long time since we have seen you. Your father does not say much, but I want you to come. So don't be too long.'

Gildas, however, never referred to the invitation. For he had a secret plan on which he had asked the Director's advice.

On a midwinter morning of blustering wind, cold rain, and driving clouds, Alexis stood sulking by a huge pile of faggots which his father and Ange—now returned from his regiment—had brought from the Dorbe Field, where they had been trimming the pollards and clearing the thorns. They had brought back the empty wheelbarrows and left the heap of faggots under the apple trees in the orchard. Ange had said :

' It's your job to heap them up, Alexis. Time's getting on, and we've got to harrow down in Bottom Field.'

Alexis had shown during the past that he had both courage and strength for work on the farm ; yet at the thought of the stack of faggots which he must build his heart so sank within him that tears came into his eyes.

Anna, who was passing, noticed his unhappy face.

' Cheer up, Alexis,' she said, ' I'll help you.'

' You can't.'

' I'll show you if I can't. I'm finished in the house, so give me a fork.'

She plunged the blue steel of the fork into the faggots, and exerting all her strength dragged the load to Alexis, who began to stack the wood in a trim heap. At the end of an hour the boy was very weary. He wiped his brow and neck with his coloured handkerchief, and in order to rest himself surreptitiously looked over at the cliff, where wreaths of fog were rising from Penmur Pool. His mother came to the orchard in search of Anna.

' You here ? ' the old woman said. ' You look tired out, and your hair's full of leaves. You're as red as a beetroot, and you're shaking all over. That's no woman's work. Come along in at once ! '

Throwing down her fork, Anna answered in a low voice :

'You're right, Aunt Marie, but though it's not woman's work, I've got to do it.'

The two women walked along together. Marie Maguern looked at her niece pityingly. Her sympathy for all her household gave her an understanding of each of them, while Anna was always frank with her.

'Why did you help him, my girl ? You know quite well it's too hard for you.'

Anna's candid eyes looked straight at her :

'I don't mind how much work I do, Aunt Marie, or what kind. But I must work.'

'Yes, I know that.'

'I shan't feel young much longer, and if I lose my looks so much the better.'

Marie Maguern was touched. Drawing nearer the girl, she said :

'God loves you.'

'Do you think so ? For I often complain.'

'He has asked you to give up more than he has some, but you've done his will, my dear. It's hard for me to give up Gildas, too. Yet our sacrifices won't be for nothing. He'll be the better priest for them.'

'Yes, I believe he will, Aunt Marie.'

They reached the house. At the midday meal the men spoke of the new stack of faggots Alexis had just finished. Jean-Guillaume said nothing at the time, but on going back to his harrowing he beckoned to his wife. As he lit his pipe he said :

'Anna seems to be getting an old woman lately.'

'Yes. Strange enough she's glad.'

'She works much more than she need do.'

His wife was silent for a moment. Remembering how little he had understood their son, she said simply :

'Perhaps she's trying to make up for the extra wages you've given her.'

Jean-Guillaume shook his head :

'She's no ordinary girl.'

'That's what I've been thinking for years, and if you listen to me she'll stay here with us while we're alive.'

Bewildered, he threw out his arms, thinking how little he understood these young people who liked to grow old.

He went to his harrowing.

One morning, less than two weeks later, when the early spring days had burst the willow-buds, the son of a neighbouring farmer, a former acquaintance of Gildas', came into the farm-yard. Still holding her duster, Marie Maguern shouted to him from the door :

'What is it—have you brought a message ? '

'That's right, Mme Maguern.'

'Let's hear it then ; you're not afraid of me, are you ? '

Taking off his cap, the boy came nearer the doorway. He said respectfully : 'I've brought a letter for you. It's from Gildas.'

'He can't have had an accident, can he ? '

'I don't think so, madam. He wrote to me and put this letter inside. He told me not to give it to anybody else except you.'

Quickly the old woman took the letter from him, and dismissing the boy sat down in the empty living-room. With a beating heart she began to read :

'DEAR MOTHER,—

'Lent is about to begin. I shall not write again until it is over. At Easter, they tell me, I am going to be allowed to wear a cassock. I have been waiting for this to come and see you. I don't know whether I shall get

permission. It will be a great favour if I do. Perhaps
father's good Christian heart will be touched when he
sees me in priest's clothes, and thinks that I shall never
wear any others. I shall tell our Superior this. He is a
man of great understanding. I am telling you, but I
know that you will keep this to yourself. How glad I'll
be if I can manage it, and if father welcomes me ! It will
be a great joy. Pray for me ! '

It was only after considerable difficulty that Gildas
obtained permission to visit Penmur. Such deviations
from the rules are not desirable and may even be harm-
ful. They tend to destroy that serenity of mind which
makes for spiritual strength. It needed a long talk with
the Superior, whose wise insight at length prompted him
to grant Gildas' request. He knew that neither caprice
nor purely filial affection impelled Gildas to ask for leave
in term-time. For more than three years previously
this young man whom God had called had with quiet
courage denied himself any visit to his old parents and
the other woman, who was still there. During those
years he had put spiritual weakness from him. Even in
the externals of dress, bearing, and accent, he had
changed from the Breton which he had been. It was
only a high motive that made him wish to visit Brittany.
The old father, seeing his son in a priest's cassock, would
surely become reconciled and forgive him the hardship
which his absence had caused.

Eventually the Superior had granted permission.

At dinner-time one morning the Abbé Gildas Maguern
entered the Penmur living-room. It was empty except
for Anna, who was laying the table. She trembled at
the sight of him, and gasped :

' Oh ! Gildas ! '

She rushed from the room, hiding her face and still carrying the plate which she had been setting on the table. She shouted :

' Gildas is here. He's back ! In his cassock ! '

She did not return.

They all came running into the room—Marie Maguern, Denise, Ange, Armandine, and last of all Jean-Guillaume. The old man faltered as he approached the group about his son.

The others made way for him. Jean-Guillaume stared intently at his son. At length, closing his eyes, he held out his arms. The young seminarist ran to him, and without a word the old man kissed him on both cheeks.

Jean-Guillaume released Gildas at last, and studied his face afresh. The father's cheeks had grown strangely white. Three times he nodded, and said at length :

' You're very much changed, Gildas.' After a short pause he went on : ' I don't know whether I'm happy or sad, but I feel all upset.'

His hands were shaking. Once or twice he muttered, but none of his mumbled words could be distinguished. The old man looked at Gildas once more, as he stood in the light streaming from the door, his hands clasped and his eyes intent as though he prayed. With his old authoritativeness Jean-Guillaume said :

' Sit down here on the right of me, Gildas ! '

' Yes, father.'

Jean-Guillaume took his seat at the head of the table as he had done every day since his wedding. Eating his meal in silence, he paid no apparent heed to the chatter

of his family, or to the tales which Gildas told them of
the war and Châtillon and Paris. As he bent over his
plate, his face was gloomier than ever. When he thought
he was unobserved, from time to time he stole quick
glances at Gildas. Then once again his only interest
seemed to be in the artichoke which he dipped in the oil
and vinegar on his plate. He could not accustom himself to the idea that this son of his, who had worked
with him on the farm, and whom he had last seen in his
soldier's cloak and leggings with a soldier's moustache,
could now be sitting here clean-shaven and in the black
cassock of a priest. While others listened, questioned,
and chattered, he could not have been more absorbed in
his own thoughts had he been considering a new lease for
Penmur or an alteration in the terms of the old.

After a while Jean-Guillaume grew accustomed to the
sight of his son's cassock, and even smiled when Gildas
said : ' If father doesn't mind, I'll tell you a story of the
holidays and about a trip I took the boys one summer,
not far from here.'

Once the old man was near to tears. Armandine had
brought in some boiled chestnuts, the last of that year.
They had been shaken down by Alexis this year, but
formerly the daring and agile Gildas had gathered them,
high in the branches. As she put the steaming plate on
the table, she said : ' You won't get them when you're
a monk.'

' A monk ? ' her brother returned with animation.
' I shall never be a monk, my dear.' And then more
gravely he went on, looking in turn at his brothers, at
Denise, and at the bright-eyed Armandine :

' My greatest wish is to lose myself in the work of a
large parish, and to stay there until I die.'

The words surprised the others, who turned instinctively towards their father. The old man raised his head and looked Gildas full in the eyes :

' How long will it be, Gildas, before you can say Mass ? '

Gildas' young laughter sounded through the house. At the merry sound of it his mother turned from the saucepan which she was hanging on its hook, while Jean-Guillaume himself was gladdened by this joyful laughter heard after so long a time, as if he listened to an old tune, and waited in pleased expectation for the next words. But Gildas, recollecting that he was under discipline, said soberly :

' I beg pardon for laughing, father, but that's such a long way off. Why, I haven't even been tonsured.'

' I know, but still how long will it be ? '

' Four years, anyway.'

' For a boy as old as you ? '

' Yes, it might be five. You see, I've got to do two years' philosophy and three years' theology. At most I shall be let off a year, though that's not very desirable.'

' What's it all for ? '

' To make me fit for my parish.'

' What parish ? '

' I don't know yet, father. It depends on what I'm given. I hope it's among the poor.'

The old man was much moved by these words. He tried to conceal his emotion as he sat gazing through the open door at the ricks which Gildas had not helped to build. The children and their mother wondered at his silence, and waited for him to speak.

Jean-Guillaume's eyes came back to his son.

' What did you say ? '

'I said : " I hope it's among the poor." I'd rather be there than anywhere.'

The father looked still more intently at him. The silence deepened. Finally the old man said :

'So you like the poor best. But that will be no change for you. What's made you want to work with them ? '

'Well, I found out here and at the war.'

'Here and at the war ? '

'Yes, at Penmur and in the Army. Do you think I didn't know when we used to plough for the widow Voilier, and those others you help out of charity ? '

His father was silent for a minute, but over his face there spread a look of happiness. The lids flickered over his grey eyes as he said :

'It's quite true, my boy, that in our family as far back as I can remember we've always done our best to help our poorer neighbours.'

Once more he stopped. They all listened as he continued :

'And now our reward is a priest in our family.'

From her place at the other end of the table Marie Maguern looked at her husband in astonishment. To herself she exclaimed :

'What a change ! To think that he should be reconciled with Gildas like this ! Why, he's almost as pleased as I am ! '

She watched Jean-Guillaume stretch across the table and take Gildas by the hand that one day would have authority to bless. She saw the old man get to his feet. He said :

'You sit in my place, Gildas, as though you were the priest here on a visit.'

Marie Maguern saw her son take the place at the top of the table. Jean-Guillaume called to Denise to bring a bottle of cider to drink the health of the Abbé Maguern. The old man himself filled the glasses ; standing up and stepping back a little, he asked them all to drink to the son who should be the honour of their house.

As they stood up, all looked towards Gildas. Already they saw him a priest at the altar, and were proud of their relationship with him. The young man was pale with emotion at the sound of the title which would not be his for four more years. There was silence round the table. Even the baby clinging to her mother's skirts was quiet. The unpeeled chestnuts and the full glasses were still on the table :

' Come along ! ' said the old man. ' Drink ! '

The chinking of the glasses was heard in the farm-yard, where a cock crowed, and several sparrows flew up from the roof, where they were looking for corn.

Jean-Guillaume was the first to set down his glass. Although he could not bring himself to say so before the younger children, he felt sharp regret for his past attitude towards Gildas. He wanted, however, to express his regret, and looking toward his wife, who was clearing away, he said :

' Your mother understood from the start. Just as she'd give a bushel of wheat to the poor, she gave her son to God.'

The idea amused Alexis and Armandine, who laughed aloud.

No one commented on the empty chair beside Denise's. The glass had been filled with the rest, and now stood full of cider.

Jean-Guillaume went on :

' You won't have long with us, my boy. Would you like to walk round the fields with your mother and me ? '

' Of course he would ! ' Marie Maguern said. ' I can't walk so well as I used to, but you can help me over the stiles.'

The remark served to relieve their heightened feelings, and they all began to laugh.

' You'll see several changes, Gildas,' his father said. ' Ange gets through a deal of work and Alexis is coming on. He hasn't much strength, but he's got brains.'

' Let's go then ! ' Gildas answered. ' I was going to suggest a walk myself.'

They started their round of the Penmur fields.

They spoke little. Rejoicing to have Gildas back, the old woman would not leave his side. Only two could walk abreast on the narrow borders by the hedges, and Jean-Guillaume walked behind them. From time to time he said in his harsh voice :

' The wheat was never finer in Four Days than this year, Gildas ! '—' D'you remember the weed in Castilly meadow that poisoned the sheep ?—Well, look at the meadow now ! '

They went by the fields of newly planted apple trees and the lucern fields, and finally came to the long meadow known as Old Cross. Here Jean-Guillaume pointed out Anna's four rows of potatoes, saying :

' Would you believe it ? She wanted to dig them herself ! '

His wife broke in hastily : ' Yes, she's a hard worker, as Gildas knows. But come along ! '

Soon they reached the boundary of Penmur. Here with one accord the three turned to look at the land which they had tilled and loved. Shaking the dust from his cassock, Gildas took his parents' hands, and said, using his childhood's mode of address :

' Mother and Father—I had better tell you now. I shan't be coming to Penmur again after this.'

' You've been little enough lately. You can't mean that you won't be coming at all ? '

' Yes. For when I'm with you all, I don't feel strong enough for my work.'

' Poor boy ! ' his mother said, while Jean-Guillaume joined in with, ' Yes—once you've put your hand to the plough, you can't look back.'

' That's what I mean, father. It's best, I'm sure. You'll come to Paris on my ordination day, won't you ? '

Marie Maguern said : ' Yes, son.' Her husband turned back his sleeve and showed his bony wrist with the remark : ' Yes, if I'm still here, but for the last year I've been breaking up.'

' You'll be here right enough, father. When the time comes, I'll tell you about the trains and where to stay. They'll give you a warm welcome at Issy, you'll see.'

' Well, time will show. But let's get back now. It's late.'

On their way home Marie Maguern allowed her husband to walk with the boy. They heard her murmuring from behind them : ' Yes, that would be best. . . . I'll have a word with her . . . he's not coming back . . . that will be best.'

On the moor they walked together, Gildas between his parents. As they came in sight of the house, his father said : ' Come and look at the oxen—you'll see more changes there ! '

As Marie Maguern left them in the farm-yard, she took Gildas by the sleeve and whispered : ' That's right. Go

along with him ! But come back when he's tying them
up. There's someone who'll grieve if you don't say
good-bye.'

There were more beasts in the stable than Gildas
remembered. They came to the four tawny oxen, which
the old man kicked gently to make them stand, partly in
honour of his son and partly out of vanity. For these
oxen had no match in the district. They were eating, and
to attract their attention Gildas said with a laugh :
' Ho-Hup, Bileux ! ' But not one of the four turned.
Gildas then called Major, but there was no Major to
answer him. Jean-Guillaume shouted : ' Here, Bruno !
Ruby ! Let's have a look at you ! ' The beasts at once
turned, pulling at their cords, and looked at the master
who was so familiar, and the man whom they did not
know.

Gildas understood even more clearly that now he had
no share in Penmur.

As his father went to feed the mare which was in
Bounce's place, he left the stable and went to the living-
room.

Only Anna was there. She stood close to the door, and
plainly was waiting for him. She was as he remembered
her. Her wide grave eyes looked full into his own. It
was hard to recognise the girl who, three hours earlier,
had been so discomfited by his cassock, that symbol of
his separation from the world.

' So here you are ! I was wondering if you would come
to say good-bye,' Gildas said with a hint of formality.

The formality hurt the girl, though this was not to be
guessed from her manner. She told herself that their
past together was finished, and that Gildas was right to
make this plain :

She said simply : ' Your mother asked me to come.'

' I'm glad. For we may not see each other again.'

' Never ? '

' I don't suppose so.'

' Aren't you going to be a rector somewhere in these parts ? '

' No, Anna. I shall be a curate and perhaps a parish priest later on, but it won't be in Brittany. I shall have to go where I am sent.'

' Yes—go where we're sent. I understand that all right. But we never see what's best for us.'

' So, you're bringing up the baby for Denise, Anna ? '

' Yes, mostly.'

' I know that you're as good as a mother to her.'

' It's easy enough to feel like a mother. And she's such a good little thing.'

' They tell me you're always hard at work.'

' Yes, we're not well off yet.'

' But you're happy, aren't you ? '

She made no answer, but gazed resolutely at him. Her eyes were clear and steady.

' Gildas, I'll tell you what I think. I don't regret that you're to be a priest, and it's a great honour for your parents. I can't set myself against God, yet it's hard to get used to it all at once. And I'm not happy very often.'

' That will come later, I know.'

' Well, you must remember that I'm thirty already. Though your father and mother treat me well, it's hard I shan't have my own home.'

Gildas looked round the living-room where they had all grown up, and said deliberately :

' I shan't either, Anna. When I'm a priest in my

poor parish, I shall be everybody's servant just as much
as you are. I shall have to make my home with others
too. But that's God's will for us both.'

' God's will be done ! '

A voice was heard outside : ' We're waiting for you,
son.'

Hastily they shook hands. Gildas saw the rest of the
family waiting by the trap. He joined them. For the
last time there were cries of : ' Good-bye, Gildas, good-
bye.' The whip cracked ; the wheels rattled over the
cobbles, and the son of the house was gone, to return no
more.

CHAPTER XVIII

FAREWELLS

DURING the five years which Gildas spent in the big
Paris Seminary he developed, from the Breton farm-boy
who had heard the secret though imperious call in his
youth, into a priest admired of his masters at S. Sulpice.
He was fashioned much as the sculptors of the Middle
Ages shaped the Calvaries at Léon or at Tréguier from
the rough granite blocks which crop through the fields.
Much time is needed to mould the unpromising material,
yet, once it is moulded, neither frost nor rain nor wind-
sown lichen can destroy the saints thus carved at the
cross-roads or in the public squares.

Impressed by his resolution, his determination to learn
and his simple warm-hearted desire to alleviate human
misery, his superiors at the Seminary compared him to a
great rock able to withstand all storms. As such a rock
endures and laughs at the onslaught of the sea, so, they
said, would Maguern endure and laugh at the temptations of life.

Tall but slight, he might well have been called a
handsome man, though strangers were impressed most
by his gravity, which was surprising in one so young.
At the beginning of acquaintance he was undemon-
strative, but when some service was asked of him he lost
his look of abstraction and his pale face glowed with

generosity. At the first mention of suffering or of misfortune his manner showed such compassion that the least observant, the most indifferent, or the most malicious were forced to say : ' What a good friend he must be ! '

Gildas himself was conscious of his power in the presence of necessity or grief ; in response to it he chose his words carefully and restrained his pitying glances, that he might not cause misunderstanding or inspire false hope.

Slowly his knowledge of human wretchedness increased with the many stories which he heard of priests' work in Greater Paris. His comrades told him of the capital's derelicts, of the gypsies who camped round the outskirts of the city, and of their rude traditions and songs. These tales were not without humour, but such humour had little appeal to Gildas. On more than one occasion he was heard to say : ' I see nothing funny in misery.' In order to become better acquainted with these pitiful cases he did voluntary work in the poor suburbs of the city during the summer holidays of 1922.

In 1923 he was tonsured ; at Christmas of that year he took the first two minor orders, and in the following year the remaining two. In 1925 he was first sub-deacon and then deacon. Finally, in 1926, on the feast of SS. Peter and Paul, Gildas Maguern became Christ's priest, thus at last fulfilling his vocation.

His parents came to Paris for the occasion. They stayed in a small hotel, which to them seemed luxurious and fabulously expensive, near the church of S. Sulpice, where the ordination was to take place. The old people were allotted seats at the long and beautiful service at which Cardinal Dubois consecrated their son. They saw

Gildas kneel upon the sanctuary steps, and as he stood
up they thought him paler and more impressive than any
of his fellows.   The tears which his mother wept then
were the sweetest of her life.

On the following day they were present at their boy's
first Mass, and received Communion from him.   Afterwards they had about an hour's talk with Gildas in the
Seminary parlour at Issy.   Though they said no word
to each other, they both murmured in their hearts :
' Now thou dost dismiss thy servant, O Lord. . . .'

Back at Penmur, it was more than a week before they
recovered from their weariness.

Shortly after the ordination they heard from Gildas
that he had been appointed curate to a working-class
parish.   He said : ' I am delighted at being sent among
these poor and ignorant folk.'

He was sent to a flat part of the country about twenty
miles south of Paris.   It was a district of small mean
houses seemingly built without plan—houses in stone,
stucco, cement or wood ;   shacks of corrugated iron ;
hovels and sheds.   Each of them had its diminutive
garden, bounded by the railway embankment ;   each was
built at the angle its owner fancied, while many straggled
along tracks yet to be made into roads, that cut their
way through fields, with few street lights and no kerbs ;
their chief traffic was builders' lumbering lorries.   After
dark the lights gave a little beauty to this ugliness :
towards the north red and green signal lights marked the
station, and from the factories long lines of yellow
windows showed where work was progressing.   Nothing
could be seen of Paris, though it lay towards the north, a
grey immensity by day and a vast red glare by night.
The only trees in the district were along the three high

roads whose triangle enclosed this wilderness of houses
set down among the wheatfields ; for the districts
outside Paris still grew wheat as they had grown it for
centuries. In queer fenceless and hedgeless fields
between the shacks the wheat had its due seasons,
though it was not easy to say from whence the harvesters
came. Although the farms were lost in this multitude of
houses, the wheat still flourished, with its cornflowers
and its poppies bending before the wind which makes
them fecund.

Gildas greeted the fields as old friends. With the
parish priest he lived in an old garage whose workshop,
after the bankruptcy of its owner, had been rebuilt as a
chapel. There were buildings on every side of it ;
roads both made and unfinished radiated from the small
square ; there were a few shops, a post office, and a new
building which called itself the town hall. It was the
nucleus of a growing town that would later develop into
an important commune. Its population increased
rapidly with every year. Gildas spent five mornings a
week in the corrugated-iron building which he jokingly
called ' The Outpost,' where he said Mass and celebrated
baptisms, marriages, and burials. He had many callers.
All who settled in these parts were needy and most were
ignorant : their need or their ignorance drove them to
the presbytery, where none was turned away and all
received a patient hearing. For there was no question of
introduction, long delay, or any kind of payment. Where
political prejudices were not too strong, men and women
alike went to Father Maguern with instinctive trust.
They would tell some pitiful tale : ' Get me a job, father.
I don't care what it is or where it is.'—' Get me work on
the railways—in the gravel pits—at the oil depôt.'—' Do

you know anybody who will give me needlework ? '—
' Can you get me leave to stop work at six instead of
seven, because it takes me an hour and a half to get
home ?   Auguste is cross having to wait so long for his
dinner, and I'm sure it's bad for his health.'—' What can
I do with my two children, father, while I'm at work ? '
—' I'm ill, father. Will you give me a letter for S.
Joseph's Hospital ? Everybody speaks so well of it.'—
' My cellar's full of water, and nobody will help me.
What shall I do, father ? '—' My creditors have taken my
furniture. Can you give me a loan for about six weeks, or
at most two months ? '—' Please, father, my husband is
dying. Can I have some holy water for him ? '

These men and women who knocked at the presbytery
door came from every province in France, while among
them was a cosmopolitan element from every country in
Europe, Asia, and Africa. The attraction of its reputed
wealth and high wages, together with the amusements to
be found there, had drawn them to Paris. Because of the
high rents in the city, they had been forced to live on its
outskirts. Many of the immigrants hated the country in
which they had taken refuge ; for they had not understood the hard work expected of them. Their hearts were
elsewhere ; they were wistful for the homes of their
childhood and for the burial-places of their forefathers.
Those who came to Gildas Maguern too often felt the
bitterness of exile. They had one illusion left : they
would yet live in Paris, and there grow rich and enjoy life.
Most of them no longer cared for their souls ; some of
them had never cared. In their faces could be seen restlessness, boredom, envy, or remorse. There were rebels
among them ; for many of those who propagated the
gospel of hate either lived or worked in the district. They

openly advocated unrest in the present, and planned violent revolution for the future.

The gaunt old woman who came to the presbytery daily to work, and who described herself as a Parisian because she had once been a charwoman in the city, tried to warn Father Maguern. She knew, she said, far more of some of his callers than he could know. Telling him that his kind heart led him away, she finished : ' It must take the good God himself all his time to love such scum as we get round here.'

' No, Estelle, you're wrong. We have only to serve him and it's quite easy.'

Yet it needed all the young Breton's faith in him who is pity and forgiveness itself to help this procession of wretched people without being overwhelmed by his own sense of sorrow. With great patience he listened to the story of their rights and their wrongs, of their demand for an eight-hour day and of their strikes to secure it. Of the greatest injustice against them they never complained, for they were unconscious of the offences committed against the divine in themselves.

Gildas had watched them as they sadly went away murmuring their thanks. He noticed that almost always, though he assisted them, such service brought small joy to these godless men. For peace of spirit was unknown to them.

In a few months his good works and his friendliness brought Gildas first the toleration and then the love of his strangely mixed flock. His height was an advantage to the young priest among these mean people. They rarely insulted him or gave him black looks. One night during the first autumn in his parish he was walking home in the mud when a man, seeing him in his priest's clothes, shouted from a doorway : ' Yah, you holy sack of coals ! ' Gildas turned and said : ' You want some coal, my poor chap ? I haven't any here, but wait a minute.'

He was back shortly stumbling beneath the weight of a sack of coal from the neighbouring depôt. He set this beside the man who had insulted him, saying : ' Here's your coal ; you'll be able to have a fire now. I must go and clean myself.'

Twice a week Gildas said Mass and took Catechism at the smaller chapel of Nôtre Dame du Roncier away from the main streets, which the parish priest had given into his charge. The children were some consolation to him, though not because of their regular attendance ; for their parents were careless in this matter. New children, however, constantly attended. At one time there were three French, two Italians, and one Slovak, who recited the catechism with the faces of cherubs and made their first pilgrimages in things of the spirit. There was a small girl, Grisèle, who though she inherited her mother's coarse features, yet had such an instinct for self-sacrifice that even her parents would say, ' She'll be a nun.' In his thought the abbé would add : ' Of the Adoration Réparatrice.' Although he encouraged them, he was half fearful of the various young people's clubs which met on Sunday evenings at the presbytery. For they were boisterous at their games and left the rooms in such disorder that they might have been the billets of a battalion. Gildas would write letters during this time ; though often his correspondence was not finished until after midnight, he never failed to write home to Penmur.

Although he did not seek them, memories of Brittany came to him often. Thus there was a succession of beautiful days during the first spring after his installation. With the mild weather the country became suddenly green. As Gildas walked along the hard, rutted road thinking of what he should say to the sick people on whom he was calling, he suddenly stopped and caught his breath. There before him was a great stretch of fine young wheat ears, through which the breeze blew with a gentle murmuring. His thoughts turned at once to his flock. Fresh from the inspiration of that sight he whispered : ' Oh, may my people be as promising one day in God's sight ! And why shouldn't they ? '

Remembrance suddenly came to him. Again he whispered : ' Even here it's good to see the wheat ! That wheat in Four Days Field ! . . .'

Four years went by.

It takes less than four years to leave imprints on human faces, whether old or young. At Penmur neither the trees nor the fields seemed to have changed : the hedges were unaltered ; the furze bushes still bloomed twice a year ; the pines on the slopes had grown imperceptibly if at all. New clouds, like those that had preceded them, threw passing shadows on fields of corn and buckwheat as they came up from the sea. As of old the hens scratched in the farm-yards, and the house-leeks slowly spread their hold upon the roof ; sunrise and sunset left their old glory upon the rushy Penmur Pool.

It was otherwise with those who lived there. None had left the farm since Gildas had gone. But Jean-Guillaume, grown bent and wrinkled, resembled one of his own gnarled trees. His arms felt weak ; his cheeks were shrivelled, and his eyes sunken. His strength was leaving him, but his courage remained unbroken. Marie

Maguern still retained a little of her youth and lively good humour, in her gestures and in her ready speech. But she rarely left the house ; she too was bent with rheumatism and limped heavily from her varicose veins. Were Gildas mentioned, shutting her eyes to cover her emotion she would say :

' Yes, our priest's doing mission work in what they call the " red " zone. I've had several letters about him, even one from His Grace of Paris, saying what a good priest he is. He always takes the Sacraments to the dying, and is seen as often as the postman going from house to house trying to convert people to the faith. He has next to nothing for himself, and even spends his holidays looking after children—the Lord knows what a plague they are ! They say he's better than any curate they've had in that parish before. I doubt whether we shall ever see him again ; we can't go to him—that means he would have to come here. But we can't ask that of him. He hasn't the time.'

At such remarks Jean-Guillaume would grow suddenly restless, and on some pretext or other would take his stick and leave the house. For he was tormented by memories of the long resistance he had maintained against what had proved to be for the benefit of his fellow-men and the honour of his own house.

Denise had grown stout with the years, and remained the grumbler she had always been. She liked to visit the town, and on returning from her shopping invariably brought back the week's gossip. Her daughter Marie, now a tall girl of fourteen, was the only child left at the farm. As fair as her Aunt Anna, already on coming from Mass on Sunday she attracted the gaze of the young farmers and of their relatives too by her beauty.

Ange Maguern now managed Penmur. He was harsh and more burly than his father. Yet his rough speech and quickness to anger concealed a lonely heart. When he was chaffed about the girl he would marry, he would merely smile, knowing that he had but to glance at any in Muzillac and she would be glad to answer his advances. So why hurry ? He liked the attentions he received, and knew he would lose them when he married.

Alexis had grown into a strong man, like his father and Gildas in appearance. He had helped to give Penmur the reputation of having the richest cornfields in Muzillac, while his own savings in the local bank steadily increased.

Anna had grown resigned. She was content to bring up her niece Marie, whom she called her daughter, and to be held of no account herself. In this she resembled many others of her race and of her faith, whether they be found in convents, in their own homes, or like herself in the homes of others. Like them, she had struggled against her rebellious youth and had come at last to peace and even thankfulness. She would soon be thirty-seven, but she was scarcely changed : her features were as fine and her head as delicately poised as in the days of her dances after the threshing, and the diadem worn by the Monks' Island women was as becoming to her greying hair as it had been when it was golden. Now there were little lines about her eyes and mouth, and her teeth were no longer perfect. She rarely went outside the farm, and was always dressed in quiet and simple clothes. She had lost her great friend, Mme Voilier, though in these days Anna seldom needed advice. Everywhere she was much loved for her great unselfishness. By 1930 her wages had risen to two thousand francs—a large sum even in post-war days. It was Alexis who now hoed her potatoes, as Gildas had done before him.

On his return one July evening of that year Gildas found his parish priest at his lodging. The old man said :

' My dear abbé, what about those holidays ? '

' I'd like a week, Father, if you could manage it. I've a friend who has asked me to . . .'

' Tell him you can't. . . . Abbé Tanguier who usually has the summer camp has fallen sick, and I want you to take it for him. You must start with the boys the day after to-morrow.'

' Where is it to be ? '

' By the sea near Arradon, Morbihan. Do you know it ? '

' It's near my own home.'

' You already know the children, or some of them at least. . . . Oh, one thing more.'

' Yes, sir.'

' I've been told by His Eminence that you are to be appointed . . .'

' Not to be a parish priest, I hope.'

' Well, much the same thing. You've to be in charge of Nôtre Dame du Roncier. It's to be made into a parish as soon as the chapel and schools and the rest of it are ready. It comes to this : the Archbishop wants me to give over a third of the parish to you ; for it gets bigger and more crowded every day. . . . As soon as you are back from the sea, you'll have to get your traps together and go over to Roncier. There's no presbytery, you know, and I don't know where you'll get lodgings.'

With a murmured *Fiat!* Gildas bent his head, and then aloud to the vicar said : ' Very well, Father.'

The young abbé started two days later for the seaside near Arradon, where for a month he was in charge of the forty odd ragamuffins who had joined the camp. He organised their work and their games and was responsible for the welfare of their souls and bodies alike. For their sake he made undue demands on both his strength and his money. At the end of the fourth week he was utterly weary. His days were a round of constant supervision of these urchins, while his nights were short and broken. Their babel was unceasing as they ran and shouted in all the abandonment of restless childhood.

On the last day Gildas telegraphed to Penmur : ' Returning Paris with boys reaching Vannes station August 29 ten p.m. meet me Gildas.'

Ten minutes before the time mentioned, Alexis drove the Penmur waggonette into the station yard. Leaving him leaning on the shaft, Anna and the old couple went into the third-class waiting-room, where they sat on a form under the dusty window. A train came in, and bored-looking passengers hurried along. Anna, who had peered through the window, turned and said : ' He hasn't come.'

She had barely sat down when the door was thrown open, and Marie Maguern cried : ' Here he is ! '

His cassock was bleached by the sea ; he looked older than they remembered ; more resolute and handsome.

' Hullo, mother and father and Anna ! It's good of you to have come all that way. But we mustn't waste time. I've only got a few minutes. The boys are locked in the reserved compartments. How are they all at home ? '

'Very well. Alexis is holding the mare, but your father is going out in a few minutes to change places with him.'

Gildas kissed his mother, who arranged her skirts and made room for him beside her at the end of the form. Anna, dressed in her working clothes, sat between her aunt and uncle, who with his bowed shoulders stared straight before him.

Marie Maguern continued :

'And how are you, son, now that you've asked after all the others ? You've got thinner.'

'That's not to be wondered at, mother. I have so much to do. I'm going to be a kind of rector in the "red" zone. The parish isn't quite made yet—it's chiefly little houses and a few fields. Still, before the month's out, I shall be in my church there.'

'Jean-Guillaume, do you hear that ? '

'Yes.'

Marie Maguern continued : 'What's the name of your parish, Gildas ? '

'Nôtre Dame du Roncier. I'll give you the address. There'll be about four thousand souls.'

'They'll be pagans, won't they, from all I've heard ? '

'Some of them, I expect, but mostly they'll have just lapsed.. There's sure to be a few good folk. They've come from all parts of the world there. I know some of them already. It'll be a hard job, but I'm determined to do all I can.'

'Yes, Gildas, we know.'

'I shall soon get old there. But that doesn't matter. If I wear myself out with them, it's all one to me, because I love them and want to see them saved.'

The old woman fumbled in her pocket, disarranging

her voluminous skirt : ' There, my boy ! A hundred francs ! I've been saving it up for you. Your father's helped me.'

Jean-Guillaume nodded feebly. She handed Gildas the note, which she had carefully folded that none might see what she gave him.

' Take care of it, Gildas ! '

' Now you give me money for them. You've done much more. Without knowing it, you reared me for them, and when you knew my secret, you gave me to God for them.'

As he spoke, the young man looked at his mother with affection and gentleness, and her heart was proud within her. In the future he would treasure this memory of his mother, and her proud eyes as she surrendered him to the poor and the unknown of Roncier.

Gildas thrust the note, still folded, into the pocket of his belt. Drawing out his watch, he said : ' Five minutes gone already ! '

Passengers came and went through the door of the waiting-room. Looking at Anna, the young priest saw that her face was resigned like his mother's :

' I see that you too have understood,' he said softly. Still more softly he added :

' You know what sacrifice means, and the joy of it.'

Anna had listened in silence, storing in her heart every word that he had said. At last she answered :

' Yes, Gildas ; as you said I would.'

' God be praised ! '

' For ever and ever ! '

There was a pause. Anna once more began to speak from her inmost heart. In solitude she had often murmured the words which now came easily to her :

' Once I felt despised because you set me aside for your vocation. It took a little time to get over that. But now, like Aunt Marie, I'm proud of our priest. You're going to those pagans. We helped to send you, and we shall have some of the merit. Don't worry yourself about any of us again. There's no need. Every time you say Mass for your flock, remember that your mother and I have a share in it.'

' That's true, and I'll pray every day for you.'

' And I for you.'

' Well, I must get back.'

His father started up from a half-doze and looked at the son whom he too had surrendered :

' I've nearly forgotten to tell you : you remember Dorbe Field ? '

' Yes, father.'

' Well, it's got on fine ! Toufféguy has got a fine crop of lucern this year. I got a hundred bushel of wheat off Old Cross, so you see Penmur's going on all right.'

Seeing that people were crowding towards the door, Marie Maguern nudged her son's arm :

' Gildas, bless us before you go ! '

They all stood up, and he gave them his blessing.

Porters hurried past, and a megaphone began to blare : ' Take your seats for Nantes, Angers, Tours, Orléans, and Paris ! '

The monitor of the camp burst into the waiting-room :

' Father, the stationmaster told me to say that there's an awful row going on with the boys. And it's time to go.'

Gildas kissed his parents and ran along the platform. From their compartments the boys leaned out of the carriage windows, and shouted as they saw him : ' Hurry up, Father ; the train's just going ! '

To the great excitement of the boys, Alexis Maguern stood on the foot-board, and for some twenty yards was carried along as he shook his brother's hand. As the train gathered speed, he jumped off, shouting his good-bye.

Gildas began to inspect the five compartments reserved for his boys. There were quarrels about the corner seats ; two of the urchins had to be fetched down from the rack, and luggage that they had piled against the window stowed under the seats. At last there was some measure of peace, and Gildas could take his seat in the end carriage, though twice he was called to settle a dispute.

He carried his Breviary ; for later when the boys slept he hoped to read his Office. The September night was clear but cold, with a slip of moon and many stars. The train passed near Muzillac, and Gildas looked eagerly at the familiar country-side. It was dark, yet he, with his country boyhood behind him, recognised the moor with its low stone walls, its clumps of furze, and the boulder-strewn slopes. The train went by apple-orchards such as he remembered well. Here and there in the distance he saw farms like Penmur, and it gladdened his heart to see fields of buckwheat glimmer white in the half-darkness. Until the last of the cornfields had vanished, he gazed wistfully at the country-side, content to leave his Breviary for a while.

His family meanwhile were on the road back to the farm. Jean-Guillaume sat beside his son, and nothing could be heard in the still night except the sharp trot of the mare. Marie Maguern, well wrapped in her shawls, made a pretence at sleep, while Anna sat huddled and dreaming in the black cloak she had worn on that

Christmas day so many years before. Filled with a sense of their spiritual victory, neither of the women spoke. They had put grief from them, both the grief of that evening's parting and their grief of past years. Quiet joy and thankfulness possessed their hearts, like a silent flood, to which they seemed to add their stream of adoration. At intervals Jean-Guillaume would say : ' Keep to the right, son ! There's a motor coming.'

Soon the train had left behind the moorland stretches with their stunted trees, the low stone hedges, the gorse and the buckwheat and the little fields. Gildas knew that now they were no longer in Brittany. He rejoiced to think that his family knew peace of soul, and that at le Roncier there were others who, because of his sacrifice of that family, would also know peace of soul. He looked at his boys as they dozed and slept. A sudden calm happiness descended on his spirit. He remembered the five words which had been the turning-point of his life : ' You shall be my priest.' He murmured the response : *Magnificat anima mea Dominum*. It was close upon midnight. He opened his Breviary. Turn to page 2

THE END